TRUCK OFF AND DIE

RILEY ODELL

CHAPTER ONE

THE CITY COOKS in the sun glowing faint behind amber smog. In the street, between megalithic monstrosities of steel and glass, a gridlock of vehicles clogs passage. Boxed-in drivers honk their horns as if this will somehow clear the way. An ambulance blares its siren with equal futility. A short distance ahead, a police car also has its siren on. Emergency response times average two hours and forty minutes.

Parker weaves among the viscous mass of people on the sidewalk, like a rat in a wriggling, shifting maze of flesh. Sweat lathers every inch of his body. In this heat, everyone is their own personal perspiration fountain. The collective odor wafts up and joins that of all the trash—an ever-growing amount the city cannot begin to keep up with—to form a vast stink, as thick and pervasive as the smog.

He unclips a water bottle from a carabiner on his belt, takes a couple of sips, then closes it back up. Has to ration. Water, even from the tap, is expensive.

"Step back, ma'am." On Parker's left, a man in a security uniform pushes away a woman who's drawn too close.

The woman pants like she's out of breath. Her bloodshot eyes flit about. Bugs crawl in the untamed jungle of her hair. She's on something, maybe the new opioid that's been in the news. "They're in the colors," she says. "Don't you see them? They're in the colors. They're in your eyes."

The security guard stares her down, unflinching. "You need to move along."

She steps toward him. He shoves her back again. Parker passes the two of them. A man barrels past in nothing but tighty-whities, shouting something incomprehensible, while another guard gives chase. Any direction Parker looks, there are guards. They're at every corner, every storefront. Private security's long since stepped in to fill the gaps left by an understaffed police department, but it feels like the guards are more prevalent than ever. More and more every year, since the start of the Great Decline.

Parker turns and enters his work building. It's just as hot inside, no air conditioning—hasn't functioned in ages. Parker's body is used to the heat, though. He's been living with it all his life.

The building's first floor is a fluorescent-lit corridor lined with doors, most leading to vacant offices. A woman lets out a shrill, terrified scream from behind a door to Parker's right. That one belongs to Dr. Shellick, a so-called orthodontist. Shellick gives his signature cackle, and the woman screams again. Parker wonders, not for the first time, how Shellick still has any patients.

Shellick's office is one of only two businesses still in operation on this floor. The other is Bildo's Dildos, four doors down from Shellick. A man in an orange rubber dildo costume stands at the entrance to the sex toy shop. The man waddles over to Parker, each step slow, labored by the heavy outfit.

"Bildo's has a mascot now?" Parker says.

"Yep, that's . . . me," the man pants. "I'm Bildo, it's . . . nice . . . to meet you!"

"Are you okay?"

"Never . . . been . . . better!"

"You sound like you're on the verge of heat stroke."

"Definitely . . . not! Would you like . . . to buy . . . a dildo?"

"Nah. I don't have a vagina, and I don't like shoving things up my ass."

"What about your mouth?"

"Sorry, no thanks." Parker makes a move toward the stairs.

"You wouldn't wanna pass on the new Turbo Dildo 3,000! It's got all kinds of crazy features! You can pleasure yourself with it, but it also doubles as a kitchen knife—"

Parker winces. "A *knife?*"

"I think you have to like, press a button so it transforms, or something like that. I'm uh, I'm pretty sure there's no way it will like, glitch and become a knife while it's in you; that would be nuts, right? You know what, forget the knife thing. It also has a built-in AI that will do your taxes for you, too, and—"

"Still no."

"Four hundred thousand! Or monthly payments of ten thousand a month."

"Becoming less interested by the second."

"Okay. Okay. How about . . . about . . . "

The man can't get the words out. He stumbles, as if dizzy.

"You do *not* seem okay," Parker says.

"Yeah, fuck this, I'm not." The man turns away from Parker and goes into the store. "Hey, boss?"

"Why aren't you selling dildos?" asks the boss, whom Parker can't see from the hallway.

"I'm dying," Bildo says. "I need some water."

"Are you serious? Do you have any fucking clue how much water costs?"

"But . . . you've got a full water cooler in your office."

"You know I make one hundred and sixteen times more than you, right? That means I work a hundred and sixteen times as hard. I *need* all that water."

"But you just sit in your air-conditioned office and—"

"Get the fuck back out there and make me my money!"

Bildo waddles back out, muttering, "This is ridiculous,

we never sell any of these things anyway, the whole thing's just a . . . " He stops as he notices Parker. "Ah, hello again, potential customer! Any chance you've changed your mind on the Turbo Dildo 3,000?"

"No," Parker says.

"Might you instead be interested in—"

The man collapses. The instant his body hits the floor, he explodes, sending out blood, bone, brains, and guts in all directions. Something that might be a spleen or a kidney hits Parker square in the face. The stench of burst bowels mixed with iron overwhelms him, and he vomits, raining last night's dinner onto the man's corpse.

For a moment, all Parker can do is stand in shock, because it's oh-God-so-horrible, disgusting, atrocious, and furthermore, how will he explain to his boss why he looks like Carrie at the prom?

The thing about Bildo's Dildos is, it's actually a front for an experimental weapons company. Although the sign by the door states, "Bildo's Dildos is NOT a front for an experimental weapons company," everyone knows that's not true. Poor Bildo here, or whatever his real name was, must have unwittingly been carrying one of those weapons on him.

A heavyset man in a suit worth a year of Parker's salary appears in the shop's door. "You *idiot!*" he bellows at his employee's corpse. "How the hell will you sell any dildos like *this?*" He spits on it. "Worthless! Worthless trash! And you—" He points at Parker. "If you're not here to buy something, go away!"

Parker wishes he'd taken that advice a minute earlier. He crosses the bloody floor to the stairs and heads up.

The building's second floor is vacant and dark. Various objects lay discarded in the hall, visible only by their outlines. Parker continues upward. The light from the first floor no longer reaches this part of the stairs, so he takes out his phone and turns on the flashlight. On the third floor, a breeze blows from somewhere unseen. Whisper-like susurrations emanate from open doors. Parker climbs to the fourth, and final, floor.

Midway down the hall is a wall vent from which the grated cover has been removed. The vent is level with the floor. Parker goes prone, then crawls inside. The narrow space is barely big enough to fit him. It's a good thing he's done this so many times he's gotten over claustrophobia.

He hits a fork in the vent system. His flashlight illuminates a red arrow pointing left. He follows it. More arrows tell him where to go so he doesn't get lost in the maze. They lead him to a room stacked full of empty boxes. A ladder descends through a hole in the floor. The metal rungs creak beneath Parker's weight as he climbs down. At the bottom, a heavy wooden door is the only way forward. The door opens to a lit room with four small cubicles—Parker's workplace.

His coworkers, Dwight, Natasha, and Janice, have already arrived. Natasha looks up from her cubicle and frowns at the sight of him. She's black-haired, petite, early thirties. "What happened to *you?*"

"A man kind of, um, exploded in front of me," Parker says.

"Well, I'm telling Vic that you were thirty seconds late, and that you came in looking like *that,*" she says. "He's not gonna be happy."

"He's not going to promote you no matter how much you suck up to him," Parker says.

"We'll see about that."

Parker wishes she'd lay off him. It's not like he's the only one here who's ever mucked something up. She holds a grudge against him in particular because of the time he accidentally ate her sandwich. The sandwiches had been identical in every way but the mustard. Natasha's obsessed with a brand of mustard she can't find often, and that had been one of the rare occasions she had some on her sandwich. The others had known about this, but Parker hadn't because it had been his second day. She'd screamed at him, called him a monster, called him the devil. Ever since then, she's been on his ass.

Parker passes the cubicles to the break room and deposits his lunch in the fridge. He returns and takes his seat. On the desk is a laminated sheet with a list of phrases and a vintage rotary phone made of wood and brass. A wired mouthpiece hangs from a cradle on the side.

"Um," Janice says. She's blonde, late twenties, tall—six two or six three, he guesses, at least a good five inches taller than himself. "You have, uh . . . " She brushes a hand over her hair.

Parker mirrors the motion on his own head. His fingers squish into a length of intestine stuck in his hair. Dry heaving, he gingerly pinches the viscera between thumb and forefinger, then tosses it in the trashcan next to his cubicle.

The phone rings. Parker lifts the mouthpiece. "Oedipus eats fried eggs at the O.K. Corral," he says.

"Pantomimed pufferfish in bloom upon the Yangtze River," the caller responds.

"May Jesus lactate in your anus." Parker returns the mouthpiece to its cradle, ending the call.

He doesn't know what any of this is supposed to mean. He just knows he's always supposed to start with "Oedipus eats fried eggs at the O.K. Corral." The caller will say something from the list of phrases on the desk. Each has a corresponding phrase Parker must respond with. Then the call ends.

Hours pass. It's harder than usual to focus because he can't stop thinking about that poor man exploding right in front of him, which isn't helped by the fact he hasn't had time to cleanse himself of the remains.

Eventually, mercifully, the lunch break arrives.

Parker gets up and walks into the break room. Its only furnishings are a long table, a fridge, and a dishwasher. Janice, Dwight, and Natasha are seated at the table.

"Okay, everyone, listen," Janice says. "I've come up with an *amazing* product idea. It's gonna make millions."

"Let's hear it," Natasha says.

Janice grins. "*Hatecense.*"

No one says anything.

"What is it?" Natasha prods after a long moment.

"So, you know how hate is really big in America? Like, bigger than ever? Anti-LGBQT, anti-black, anti-this and that. And what else is big? *Incense.* Like, the world's so crazy, you've got tons of people getting into meditation and stuff to keep themselves sane. And they also use incense to like, block out the shitty smells that are everywhere now. So, here it is: incense that smells like *hate.*"

"Just because two things are both popular doesn't mean they'll be as popular if you combine them," Parker says. "In this case, those two things are literally antithetical to each other. Hate is based on anger, whereas meditation is meant to *calm* the mind, eliminating those negative emotions. And what the hell does hate smell like, anyway?"

Janice huffs. "Well, *I* think it's a good idea."

"Parker's right," Dwight says. "Leave it to a woman to think up something so dumb."

"*Excuse* me?" Janice says.

"Oh, here we go again," Natasha says, rolling her eyes. "Let me guess, Dwight. Another woman turned you down."

"She didn't give me a *chance.* I sent her a message on match.com that said, 'Hey, you look fucking ugly.' She responded calling me an asshole and then blocked me!"

"Uh, because the literal first thing you said to her was that she was ugly?" Janice says.

"She wasn't actually ugly. That's not the point. If you compliment a woman, she'll tell you, oh, that's so sweet, you're so cute, but she's just stringing you along. You already got tossed to the friend zone the moment you said she's pretty or thought something she said was funny. Because, see, that's not what women want. They want macho·male bad boys who treat them like dirt—"

"Bzzt," Natasha says, mimicking a buzzer. "Wrong. I'm a woman and no, I don't like to be treated like dirt."

"Bzzt yourself," Dwight says. "We both know that's not true. It can't be true because if it were, there'd be no reason a nice guy like me shouldn't be able to—"

Natasha snorts. "I mean, if we wanna talk about dishonest self-assessments, that's the mother of 'em all."

"Fuck you," Dwight spits. "You women do nothing but treat us like shit, oppress us, torment us. We have no rights—"

"Seriously? Where do you live, Opposite Land? You have way more rights than—"

"Men don't even have the prerogative to have a little fun!" Dwight screams.

Natasha blinks. "Uh, what?"

"When Shania Twain says it's the best part about being a woman, the implication is *clearly* that men do not have the same right," Dwight says.

"Are you seriously basing your understanding of reality on the lyrics to an old song?"

Dwight pounds the table. "It's *facts!* Men aren't even allowed to *enjoy* themselves!"

Parker's had enough of this conversation. He retrieves his sandwich from the fridge and prepares to leave the room, to eat at his desk or maybe even in that room with all the boxes, away from the others.

Janice stops him. "Come on, Parker. Stay with us for once."

"No, thanks," he says.

"Why are you always running off to eat somewhere else? Are we boring? Is that why you don't want to talk to us?"

"Talk? You're just arguing."

"We can talk about other things. Like, I dunno, the weather."

"The extreme heat?"

"No, like, other weather."

"The smog? Acid rain?"

"Ugh! You are such a *downer!*"

"Yep, that's me. I'll see you all after lunch."

He leaves the room. Behind him, Dwight starts in on something else misogynistic, but then he screams. "My *nose!*"

"Remember what I said last week? I told you I'd break it if you kept saying shit like this."

Parker sits at his desk. He eats his sandwich, which tastes like blood since he still hasn't had a chance to wash himself off, as the others continue to argue in the break room.

After several minutes, Dwight steps out. "I'll bet *you* agree with me," he says to Parker. Blood drips from his nose down his face and onto his shirt. "That society's problems are all because of women."

Parker groans.

"It's obvious when you look at it. Society has been on a straight downhill trajectory for the last century and a half, and it lines up perfectly with the expansion of women's rights. Women's right to vote, 1920. 1964, the Civil Rights Act prohibited discrimination against women in the workplace. 1972—"

"Why exactly do you think I would agree with you about any of this?"

"You seem like a lonely person. I figured you've probably been rejected by a lot of women, too."

"I'm alone because I choose to be alone."

That clearly doesn't compute for Dwight, who looks more confused than a hungry cow on Astroturf. "Why would you *choose* that?"

"I don't think that's any of your business."

"You wanna know why *I'm* alone? Because women are too stupid to differentiate—"

Dwight implodes, collapsing into a spasming, flesh-colored distortion in space, like a tangle of glitching polygons in a videogame. The distortion lets out an ear-piecing scream.

Their boss, Vic, steps from his office opposite the break room. "The hell is going on?" he asks, stifling a yawn.

"Vic!" Natasha runs out of the break room. "Vic, Parker came in thirty seconds late today, and he's covered in *blood!*"

"Parker!" Vic crosses his arms over his grimy white wifebeater. "That is not an appropriate aesthetic for the workplace! And we have talked about your tardiness problem before."

"You just slept through half the day," Parker says.

"I wasn't sleeping. I was—" He winces. "Ow, *fuuuuck!*"

Headache, probably. Vic is almost always hungover.

Vic isn't the sort of person who should be in charge of a business. The thing is, though, Vic has a lot of children. After the world's population entered decline for the first time in recorded history—known as the "Great Decline"—the United States government incentivized procreation by offering special benefits to anyone with three children or more. Vic has ten, and those are just the ones he knows about. He's always boasting about all the condomless sex he used to have in college before he dropped out.

What qualities might make a man fit for company leadership? Integrity? Strong work ethic? None of that matters anymore. Vic raw-dogged his way into management. That's the norm now.

"Anyway," Vic says, "I wasn't sleeping, and I don't want you talking back to me like that, understood? And if you're late one more time, there will be consequences. Natasha, thank you for informing me. That earns you another gold star."

Natasha sticks her tongue out at Parker, as if getting a gold star somehow proves Parker wrong about how sucking up won't land her a promotion. A gold fucking star. What are they, kindergartners?

"Oh, right, and the other reason I came out here," Vic says. He gestures to the Dwight-thing, which hasn't stopped screaming the whole time, not even to take a breath. "What is this thing that's making all this racket?"

"It's Dwight," Parker says.

Vic squints. "Doesn't look like him."

"He—I don't know. He was just standing there, talking, and then he imploded."

"How?"

"I think it's Bildo's Dildos again."

For weeks, Bildo's Dildos has been using Parker and his coworkers as live test subjects. Parker nearly lost a limb to a rubber cube that bounced around the room before it burst and shot spikes in various directions. A fake toaster sprayed yellow gas in Janice's face that temporarily turned her into a hedgehog. Cube and toaster both had the same initials engraved—B.D.

"What?" Vic says. "No, don't be stupid. They make dildos, it's right there in the name. Why would they make something that does . . . this?"

"Because they're an experimental weapons company," Parker says.

Vic snorts. "Come on, it says right on their door that they are *not* an experimental weapons company. I'll bet it's aliens."

"Definitely." Parker nods. "Those darn aliens don't know when to quit."

"Well, get back to work," Vic says, yawning again. "Those phones aren't gonna answer themselves. And Dwight?"

Dwight continues screaming.

"We've talked about you slacking off on the job," Vic says. "You're fired."

Vic returns to his office, shutting the door behind him.

CHAPTER TWO

PARKER STANDS AT the crowded subway platform and waits for the train.

A man walks to the thick yellow warning line by the tracks. He steps onto the line and sways like a reed in the wind. Parker's stomach churns. The man is going to fall.

Dozens watch, but no one moves to help him. Parker approaches the man with caution, worried any sudden movement might startle him, make him lose his balance. Gently, Parker takes the man's hand and directs him away from the line.

"Be careful," he says. "That's a good way to get yourself killed."

The man screeches like a hyena and runs off—*away* from the tracks, thankfully. Is *every*one in the city high nowadays? Not that Parker can blame anyone who's chosen to break up with reality by way of drugs. Reality's not the greatest place to be these days.

From the tunnel comes the roar of an approaching train. Like a massive metal snake, it emerges, tearing past the platform in a rush of wind and sound.

Several moments pass and a second train approaches. Overheated brakes unleash a banshee scream. The train stops. Ads for various products plaster its stainless-steel sides. There's one for women's cosmetics, one for a weight-loss program, one for a weight-*gaining* program, one for erectile dysfunction. And of course, the usual ads shouting doom and gloom about the Great Decline, urging everyone to churn out more children.

The doors open, and Parker steps into a mass of people so thick they're practically melded together. Like sardines in a can, as the old saying goes. It's not really a saying people use anymore. Sardines, like most fish, are extinct.

The train jolts into motion. Parker falls against a woman and she shouts, "Hey! Mind my personal space!"

She must not have received the memo. Like sardines, the concept of personal space no longer exists.

Parker's apartment complex is in a sad state of affairs. Built in the nineteen-seventies, if it were human, it'd be an octogenarian. The metaphor's apt; by any metric, this is a building at the end of its life. With its sagging gutters and cracks spiderwebbing its rotted wood façade, it appears abandoned—and should be.

Sadly, there aren't any better options for normal folks. Any living space which can boast such luxury features as "Not going to make you horribly sick from living in it" or "Not at risk of collapsing any minute" has rent prices in the stratosphere. No, past that—deep space.

Parker removes his backpack, unzips it and withdraws a respirator mask. He fastens the front end over his nose and mouth and pulls the strap over his head. Ensuring the mask is secure, he enters the building. No need of a keycard or such: Security, too, is for the rich. Parker takes a left down a hallway lined on either side with doors. His feet sink into the soft carpet. There's never actually been a carpet installed here, not by humans—this one is nature's handiwork. It's made of mold, not fiber. A long white coating of mold that stretches the length of the hallway.

And it's not just the floor. No surface remains untouched by the blight. There are many different kinds, different species. Some are orange and thin, crust-like;

some are more robust, soft to the touch like animal fur; some are black like soot. All of them are a health hazard. Hence the mask.

The stairs are covered with fungus as well. Parker takes them to the second floor. Here, near the end of the hall, is the nexus of the mold outbreak. It's swelled to fill the hallway, a lumpy green-and-white eldritch mass with wriggling fungal tentacles. It's blocked access to the rooms at the end of the hall, and if it grows much bigger it'll block Parker's as well.

Mrs. Plymouth, Parker's elderly neighbor, steps out of her room. Holding a slab of raw meat, she approaches the mold abomination. "Hello, Milton," she coos, as one would talk to a pet. "How are you? Mommy got you a treat."

Mrs. Plymouth has lived alone ever since her husband died seven years ago. Old widows like her are often known to collect cats and get called crazy cat ladies. She's a crazy *mold* lady. Treats "Milton," as she calls it, like it's the most precious thing in the world. Poor woman suffers from dementia, but she has no one left to help her in her dotage.

Mrs. Plymouth extends the meat to Milton. This next part shocked Parker when he first saw it happen, but he's seen it a dozen times now. The mold stretches out toward the meat and a hole like a mouth opens in its fibrous surface. Mrs. Plymouth presses the meat inside. The hole closes back up and the mold retreats.

"That's a good boy, Milton," Mrs. Plymouth says. She pets the mold.

It makes a sound Parker would call purring if he was insane enough to think mold could purr. He doesn't know what that sound is and he doesn't like it. He wishes they could bring in a truckload of hydrogen peroxide to kill the mold, even if Mrs. Plymouth would lose her beloved Milton. It's just no good letting stuff like that grow unfettered.

Parker unlocks the door to his room, steps inside and closes it again, locks it. The room's small enough that his bed takes up a quarter of the space, and the stove, counters and fridge take up most of the rest. A large window occupies the back wall, looking down onto the filthy street. To the left of the bed is a door to the bathroom. Parker goes in and strips down—throwing his unsalvageable clothes in the trash can—and turns on the shower. He doesn't usually take showers, opting instead to wash off as best he can in the sink—the water's too expensive, and there are use restrictions. But nothing short of a full shower will do for washing off all this gore.

The water that sprays from the faucet has a yellowish color, like piss. Maybe it *is* piss, for all he knows. It's scalding hot at first, then it's icy cold, but after a moment of fiddling with the knobs, he finds a temperature somewhere within the realm of tolerable. He steps in, washes himself thoroughly, then looks in the mirror to make sure he got it all. He can't see any, so that's one nightmare over with, at least.

His stomach rumbles as he puts on new clothes. He opens the fridge and bends to look inside, just in time to catch a mutated green rat nibbling on one of his carrots.

"Hey!" Parker makes a grab for the rat, but it phases through the back wall of the fridge and disappears.

Great. They can go through walls now, apparently, which means it's open season on all his food. He might have to start laying traps.

The carrot's not the only casualty. The rat tore large chunks out of meat and other vegetables, as well. That means Parker will have to return to the store sooner than he expected. The rat might as well have eaten a chunk out of his paycheck.

Some food looks like it hasn't been touched by the rat. Parker picks out an intact carrot and eats it, then closes the fridge. He turns to his bed and sweeps the mattress and blankets clear of all the little brown cockroaches gathered there, dead husks and live ones both. He's put down dozens of roach traps, sprayed gallons' worth of insecticide, and still there are always more of them. Once finished, he lays down and settles into the pillow.

Slowly but surely, despair settles in with him.

It's like this most evenings. Once he's escaped the distractions of work and everything else, and there's nothing left to keep him from his thoughts. When his thoughts are freed, they tend to come together and stick to one another until they've formed a great and terrible weight at the pit of his being. It's worse today, as the horrors from earlier still haunt him. The exploding man. Dwight becoming . . . whatever that was he became. Even an asshole like Dwight didn't deserve an end like that.

Parker used to have medication for these episodes, evidenced by the graveyard of orange pill bottles scattered around his floor. Used to, until insurance stopped paying for it, and he in turn stopped paying for insurance. The medication had never worked well, but it had been better than nothing.

Sometimes, when things get like this, Parker writes. In elementary school, when most kids had only the vaguest notion of what they wanted to be when they grew up, Parker knew. From the day he first put pen to paper, he never had a doubt in his mind. In college, he majored in creative writing. By the time he was twenty-three, he'd already finished a book and begun shopping it around to agents and publishers. None wanted it, so he tried self-publishing instead. The day that book went up on Amazon, looking snazzy with its professionally-designed cover, Parker felt on top of the world. Fortune was about to come his way.

The book only ever sold twenty copies. At least five of those were bought by his mom.

He didn't give up. He'd been ill-prepared, had failed to understand the realities of the field. For some reason, his college writing professors had never taught him a thing about what the *business* side of writing looked like. He'd resolved to write a second book and try again, this time with more knowledge of how to sell it.

That was in 2043. Parker never finished the book, because in 2044 the government outlawed fiction writing—as well as art, music, and all other creative endeavors. In other words, pretty much every damn thing that made human existence worthwhile.

It wasn't that those things no longer existed. Such things were still made, but by artificial intelligence, not people. The government justified it by claiming there was a catastrophic worker shortage across all the industries which, as they put it, actually mattered. Society could no longer afford to have people "wasting their time" on such "fatuous undertakings," they said.

Those industries that "actually matter," however, were also purging human workers to be replaced by machines. Increasingly, humans and their abilities aren't needed or wanted *any*where. The streets run rampant with homelessness, while politicians in their cushy castles complain the problem could be solved if only people *wanted* to work.

That doesn't stop Parker from writing, though motivation is scarce since there's zero chance anyone else will read it. He's heard of secret forums on the internet where people share creative work, but he doesn't like the risk. At least one such forum was shut down in a high-profile case, resulting in mass arrests. Some of those people are still in jail. Even writing in private, never sharing it, is a risk, but not to the same degree. People theorize that the government spies on everyone's computer activity, but if that were true, Parker'd be behind bars already.

He picks up his laptop from the floor, unfolds the screen and opens a new document in Kroger Word—formerly Microsoft Word, before Kroger bought Microsoft back in 2039. The relentless absurdification of capitalism throughout the last few decades has led to many nonsensical acquisitions like this.

The cursor continues to blink. Parker can't think of a

single thing to write. Actually, that's not true. He could write about the deaths he witnessed today. That could help him get them out of his head. But it just feels impossible. It's too big. No words can properly describe those events. And because words can't do them justice, it feels like the very act of putting them to the page diminishes them.

A cartoon image of a corncob with googly eyes appears at the bottom right corner of the screen. Parker groans.

"Looks like you're struggling to get started," says Corny the corncob, who sounds like Samuel L. Jackson.

Someone at Kroger wanted to bring back the old Microsoft Word mascot known as "Clippy," but as something more reflective of the Kroger brand. Kroger owns supermarkets, and supermarkets sell corn. Connection enough, apparently.

"It's okay, we all have our 'off' days," Corny says. "Let me try helping you out. A good word to start with is 'fistula.' Another you might try is '*floccinaucinihilipilification.*'"

"Go away," Parker mutters.

Corny's googly eyes narrow to a glare. "Listen, motherfucker, I'm just trying to help here."

"I don't need any help."

"It sure looks like you—"

A three-dimensional image of a black sedan pulls into the center of the screen and stops. The back window rolls down, and the barrel of a machine gun pokes out. The gun thunders, pumping bullets into Corny, who spasms, spraying blood. The gunfire ends, Corny falls, and the sedan speeds back offscreen, back window rolling up as it disappears from sight.

Then the screen shuts off. Sensing wetness on his fingers, Parker lifts his hands. Bright red blood wells up between the keys and washes over the keyboard. The USB ports and speakers are bleeding, as well.

"Damned planned obsolescence," Parker grumbles.

He picks up his phone and opens the internet, checking

the news. The top story is about a giant trash monster that's risen from the ocean and is attacking New York City. The next is about a man who claims to have seen the face of Jesus in a spectrogram of his fart.

Heat tingles in Parker's loins, libido asserting itself. Not in reaction to the article, per se; this sort of thing strikes at random, never showing rhyme nor reason. In the address bar, he navigates to Pornhub.com for every lonely man's favorite pastime. He clicks a video with a hot woman in the thumbnail. The video loads and begins to play, but instead of the woman advertised, two blocky metal robots grind on each other with mechanized moaning sounds. Parker exits the video, tries another. It's the same thing. Looks like the porn industry finally hopped on the trend of ditching human workers for artificial substitutes. Couldn't they at least have tried to make the robots *look* human?

Google images will have to do. Parker heads there, thinks a moment, and types "college girls in bikinis" in the search bar. Dozens of images flood the screen, but not one single photo of a real woman—only AI-generated garbage. Eyes like runny eggs with black yolks; limbs too long, as if stretched out on a torture rack; misshapen fingers bunched in groups of four, six, seven, nine. Parker scans the lineup, searching for just one imitation convincing enough to fool his penis. He finds one, a blonde in a pink bikini who could *almost* be mistaken for human if it weren't for whatever the heck was happening with her ear. That's not too bad, he can just pretend it's a birth defect. He unzips his pants, takes his flaccid member in hand and ogles the fake woman's face, tits and crotch until he goes hard, then begins to stroke.

His phone rings right as he's getting to the good part. He curses, stuffs himself back into his pants and answers.

"Hello, am I speaking to Mr. Haywood?" the man on the other line asks.

"That's right," Parker says.

"Good evening, Mr. Haywood, my name is Hank. I'm

calling from the U.S. Department of Fertility and Population Expansion."

"The . . . what?"

"You haven't heard of us? We've only recently been established. You're probably unaware of the law Congress passed yesterday."

"Yep."

"Federal law now states that all Americans over the age of eighteen must produce a minimum of two offspring, or face a minimum of thirty years in prison."

"You can't be serious."

"Dead serious, sir. If I were a monkey, my name would be Serious George."

A cockroach crawls onto Parker's arm. He brushes it off. "Did someone at my work put you up to this? Vic, maybe?"

"I'm sorry?"

"I've had a shitty day. Not to mention, I was in the middle of something important. I'm not interested in prank calls."

"Doing the hanky-panky with your hand is not 'something important.'"

"I was—I was making dinner."

"We know you, Mr. Haywood. Data says there's a ninety percent chance you were in the middle of that thing I mentioned."

"I need to check the stove."

Parker hangs up. He focuses back on the AI blonde and resumes pleasuring himself. The phone rings again, same number. He lets it go to voicemail.

It rings a third time.

"Listen," Parker answers, "Stop calling me. I'm blocking—"

"Stay on the line, or you'll be arrested for refusal to speak to an agent of the United States government."

"I told you—" Parker brushes off another cockroach. "I told you I don't believe that."

"Look up the number I'm calling from. I'll wait."

Parker Googles the number. It really *is* the number for the for the U.S. Department of Fertility and Population Expansion.

"You're serious," he says.

"Serious as Serious Texas Barbecue."

"That law is completely—"

A brown hand swats the phone away from Parker. Thousands of roaches have combined to form a humanoid mass at the foot of the bed.

"You, Parker, have massacred too many of our kind," says the hideous being, its voice a dry crackle, like autumn leaves in the wind. "We have united to have our revenge. We are a god of cockroaches. You may call us the Cock King."

Parker snorts.

"What is funny?" the Cock King asks.

"Never mind."

"If you've any last words, say them now."

Parker reaches beneath his bed and picks up his can of Black Flag insect-killing spray.

"Insect killer?" the Cock King says. "That will not—"

Parker presses down on the can's black top. A jet of chemicals assaults the roaches. They spew a horrid shriek as the liquid dissolves their compound body. A small mountain of roach carcasses coalesces on the floor. Parker picks the phone back up.

"Hello?" Hank says. "Mr. Haywood, are you there?"

"Sorry, I ran into a bit of a pest problem. That law is completely ridiculous. You can't force people to have children if they don't want to."

"You are aware, I'm sure, that we are in the middle of an unprecedented low population crisis."

"Tell that to my daily commute," Parker says. "And anyway, I've got questions. For starters, what if I can't have children?"

"We've already tested your sperm. You're fertile."

"You've tested my sperm? *How?*"

"We obtained one of your discarded masturbation socks."

"That's gross."

"Don't worry about finding a partner to do the deed with. We've selected a woman for you based on a sophisticated matching algorithm. Further details have been sent to your email. Do you have any more questions?"

"Yeah, about five hundred—"

"Just kidding, I don't actually have any more time to speak with you. Goodbye."

Hank ends the call. Parker opens his email and checks his unread messages. He's got a dozen of them, mostly spam. Penis enlargement, breast enlargement, ass enlargement. Something from a Nigerian "prince." Something from an Egyptian "prince." Something from the prince of a country that doesn't exist.

He finds it, fifth down on the list. "OPEN IMMEDIATELY: Important Partner Information!" Parker opens it.

Dear Parker Haywood,

In accordance with the newly-passed Population Expansion Act, you have been assigned a sexual partner. Your partner is Mia Harper, thirty-one years old, phone number 555-868-9100. Please reach out as soon as you are able. Sexual contact must occur by 5pm, October 5th. Failure to have intercourse within this timeframe will result in prison. You will engage in regular daily relations until Mia passes a pregnancy test. Failure to copulate as scheduled will result in prison. Contraceptive tools and methods such as, but not limited to, condoms, birth control pills, pulling out, or castration are illegal according to the Population Expansion Act, and suspected use of these methods will prompt investigation. If you are found to be in violation, you will go to prison. If you or Mia are found to have made an attempt, successful or otherwise, to terminate her pregnancy, we will execute an aggressive regimen of behavioral reconstructive therapy designed to align you with society's needs and values.

Your cooperation is appreciated.
Sincerely,
The Department of Fertility and Population Expansion

Parker opens the attachment. A photo of a semi-truck appears on his screen. He searches the picture for the woman who's supposed to be there, but can't find her. She isn't beside the truck, isn't inside, isn't hiding underneath. The only thing that's odd about the truck itself is the big face on the front of the cab. Not a real face Photoshopped on, but made of metal like the rest of the truck. A woman's face, with blue eyes, rosy lips, and brown hair. The truck's grille pokes through her open mouth, painted white to resemble teeth.

Surely this "Mia Harper" isn't . . .

They've sent him the wrong photo by mistake. Even the government can't believe a human can reproduce with a truck. Can they? Actually, he's not sure.

Parker closes out of his email and dials the number provided. After three rings, a woman picks up. "Hello?"

"Uh, hi. Is this Mia Harper?" Parker asks.

"It is. May I ask who's calling?"

She doesn't *sound* like a semi-truck.

"My name's Parker," he says.

"Oh, hi! I've been informed about you. My new partner, right?"

"I suppose so."

"Are you free tomorrow at five-thirty?"

"Yeah." Parker works nine-hour days, six days a week. Tomorrow's his day off.

"There's a nice coffee shop at Jensen and 8th. Zane's. Ever been there?"

"No, but I'm fine with that if that's where you want to meet."

"Cool! I'll put it in my calendar. I look forward to meeting you!"

"Uh, yeah. Likewise. See you then."

"Bye."

She hangs up.

God, that felt awkward. At least she sounded nice. Maybe this won't be so bad.

Who's he kidding? It doesn't matter how nice she is. This is the last thing in the world Parker wants to do.

CHAPTER THREE

Z ANES CAFÉ IS bustling, with about thirty people chatting, drinking and eating pastries in the small space that looks about as clean as a gas station bathroom, and smells like one, too. Everything appears appetizing enough, but the look of disgust on a man's face as he bites into a donut tells a different story. More donuts, along with scones and Danishes and other sweets, are arranged on shelves behind a glass counter at the back.

"Yoohoo!"

A woman waves to Parker from across the café. She bears an uncanny resemblance to that face on the truck, but is definitely—as far as he can tell—a human. Parker approaches her.

"Mia?"

"Yeah. You're Parker?"

"Yep, that's me."

Mia takes a sip of her coffee. "Let's cut to the chase. If I'm going to sleep with you, I'd like to get to know you first. So, tell me something about yourself."

"Uh, something about me? Well, I work in a—"

"Yo, dude," a barista calls out from behind the counter. A woman with purple hair and a nose ring. "You can't sit there if you're not gonna order anything."

"That's a rule?" Parker asks.

"I didn't know," Mia says. "I always order something when I come in."

"We're not running a charity here, giving away free

seating to anyone who wants it," the barista says. "We've gotta make money."

"Okay, okay, I'm coming." Parker stands and walks to the counter.

"I recommend the caramel latte," Mia says.

"Okay, a small one of what she said," Parker says.

"You got it. Fifteen dollars," the barista says.

"*Fifteen?* Do you have anything cheaper?"

"You mean do we have a size smaller than small? Uh, no."

Parker grumbles, but pays for the drink.

"Name?" the barista asks.

"Parker."

The barista nods and he returns to his seat.

"You were about to tell me something interesting about yourself," Mia says.

"Right. I work in a call center."

Mia scoffs. "*Work*. Why is *work* the first thing that comes to anyone's mind?"

"Sorry?"

"What does what you do for a living tell me about who you are as a person? Especially something as boring as a *call center?*"

"To be fair, it's a pretty interesting call center. We use these old-timey rotary phones, and—"

"But do you like doing it?"

"No. I hate it."

"Then it tells me nothing about you. It's just something you *have* to do. Tell me instead what you *like* to do. Your hobbies."

Hobbies? Parker knows why his mind went straight to his job. He doesn't have anything else to say about himself. He doesn't have hobbies. He used to—reading and writing, mainly. All the new AI-written books are garbage, but stuff written by humans before the law changed is still accessible. Parker used to enjoy everything from Brandon Sanderson to Herman Melville. Now, he can't think of the last time he read a book. A year ago? More? It's been even longer since he last finished writing anything.

He can't tell Mia he's a writer. She may report him to the police. He doesn't know what she'd stand to gain from doing that, but he's pretty sure that confessing to illegal activity isn't advisable on the first date. Not that this *is* a date, nor does he want it to be. It's a mandatory meeting.

That leaves two options: Make something up, or tell the truth. The truth being that he spends most of his free time online, watching inane YouTube and TikTok videos, scrolling endlessly through Facebook posts from people he's never met or hasn't spoken to in years, and looking at pictures of cats. He doesn't find particular joy in any of this, but it's easy and it's mindless, allowing him to go hours without thinking about anything else. It doesn't help his depression, but it doesn't make it worse.

That, and porn.

"Did you fall asleep over there or something?" Mia asks.

He has to give her something. Anything. Why *not* tell the truth? Again, it's not like this is a date. He's not trying to impress her, doesn't *need* to impress her. Advancement to the next stage is already guaranteed. What does it matter if she thinks he's a loser?

Because he doesn't *want* to be thought of as a loser.

"Fucker!" the barista shouts.

Parker glances over to see who, or what, the barista is angry at. She's looking right at him.

"Fucker," she says again. "Your drink's ready."

"My name's *Parker*," he says.

"Sorry. I must've misheard."

"Sure, you did."

Parker stands and walks to the counter. Behind the counter, a machine dings and fires a lidded cup of coffee at him. He yelps, but manages to catch it. "The hell!"

"Sorry," the barista says. "The machine's supposed to have a robotic arm that reaches out and hands you the coffee, but it doesn't work properly."

"Fix it, then!"

"No time for that."

"Whatever." Parker sits and prepares to take a sip of his coffee. He stops.

The drink smells like gasoline mixed with sewage, and is viscous, like maple syrup.

"You have to drink it," the barista says.

Parker gapes at her. "That's a *rule?*"

"If you're sitting there not drinking your coffee, that sends the message to other customers that something's wrong with it. So, if you want to be in here, you drink it."

"Something *is* wrong with it! I am not drinking this . . . this *sludge!*"

Mia rolls her eyes. "Just drink it. It's good."

"But—"

"I don't want to get kicked out of here. You just have to take a sip."

Fine. One sip. Parker lifts the cup to his lips. He nearly gags from the stench alone, but maybe it tastes better than it smells.

He sips, and spews the drink onto the floor.

"That's *it!*" the barista shouts. "Get the fuck out of here! You're making our coffee look like shit!"

"It *is* shit!" Parker shouts back. "And you're the one screaming expletives at a customer! How do you think *that* makes you look?"

"*Get! Out!*"

Parker storms toward the café entrance. Another customer is called to the counter, and the machine shoots a drink directly into her face. She screams—the liquid must be scalding. Parker's was an acceptable temperature, but the shitty machine must heat the drinks inconsistently.

"You get out, too!" the barista shouts at the screaming woman.

Parker leaves the café and nearly collides with a man, who shouts at him to watch it. The sidewalk is crammed with people, as it always is.

Mia joins him, latte in hand. "Way to go," she says, glaring.

"I'm sorry," he says.

Her glare becomes a smile. "Don't worry about it."

Just like that, she went from angry to smiling? Maybe she'd faked being angry in the first place?

"What the hell is *in* that coffee?" he asks.

"Oh, you know. Coffee beans, gasoline—"

"*Gasoline?*"

"Yeah. They substitute gas for water because gas is cheaper."

He'd think she was joking if he hadn't smelled and tasted it for himself. "Isn't gasoline poisonous?"

"They use some kind of chemical process to make it safe for consumption. But it still has all the necessary nutrients. That's why I come here instead of other coffee shops. The others still use water."

"Nutrients? What nutrients does *gas* have?"

"None, for you. In my case, it's the only thing that nourishes me."

"That . . . that doesn't make sense."

She cocks her head. "Didn't the government send you my picture?"

"They sent me a picture of a semi-truck."

"Yes, that's me. I'm half truck."

Parker laughs.

Mia's brow furrows. "You don't believe me."

"How can you be a truck?"

But then he thinks about the picture, and how much it looked like Mia. It wouldn't be the first time he's encountered a woman who's not fully human—not that he wants to think about that.

"If you don't believe me, I'll show you," Mia says.

"I believe you," Parker says.

"Oh. Good."

"So, you're able to turn into a truck at any time? Like a Transformer?"

Mia's hand goes to her hip, pulls something free, and Parker barely catches a glint of steel before the point of a knife's mere inches from his eyeball. He screams, stumbles backward and crashes into a pedestrian. The pedestrian, a man, shouts a string of obscenities and plants his fist in Parker's cheek. Parker falls to the ground. Mia's on him in seconds, straddling him like they're about to screw. She holds the knife at his throat. Throughout all this, she's kept the latte in her other hand, spilling not so much as a drop.

"I am *not* a cartoon," she hisses.

"I—I'm sorry," Parker gasps. His heart pounds. Is this how he dies? Killed for a stupid, offhanded comment?

Mia withdraws the knife, returns it to its sheath. She stands. "It's okay."

She wasn't faking before. She really is this unpredictable.

She offers him a hand. "I'm sorry I flew off the handle like that. It's just, in school, I got bullied a lot. And that's how they'd tease me, saying I was a Transformer. Oh look, they'd say, there goes Optimus Prime. Which is stupid, because Optimus Prime's a guy. There aren't any female Transformers that can turn into semi-trucks."

Parker takes her hand and she helps him up.

"Now I've told you something about myself," Mia says. "So, let's get back to your answer."

Drat. Parker tries to think of something that will make him sound interesting, but he's taking too long to answer, and she's furrowing her brow again. What will she do if she doesn't get a response? Cut off his feet? Set him on fire? Sic a honey badger on him?

"I like honey badgers," he blurts out.

"Honey badgers?"

"Yeah. They're, uh, they're cool."

"Neat. I dig it." She takes a last drink of her latte, then tosses the cup into a nearby trashcan. "Okay. Time to get down to business."

Outside his apartment complex, Parker takes out his mold mask and hands it to Mia.

"What's this?" she asks.

"You'll see when we go inside," he says. "You could probably get ten thousand different diseases from the air in there. I doubt I'm living past my forties."

She puts the mask on. "Don't you have one of your own?" she asks.

"I just have the one."

"And you're giving it to me? That's sweet."

He leads her inside. "Real homey, isn't it?" he says.

"It's not a problem," she says. "I live in a parking lot."

Mrs. Plymouth is attending to her mold-pet Milton on the second floor. She smiles when she sees Mia. "Ooh, Parker's got a lady friend?" she asks. "Never thought I'd see the day."

"Just a friend," Parker says. He opens his apartment door and leads Mia inside.

"Don't have *too* much fun," Mrs. Plymouth says.

Parker closes the door. "Well, this is it."

"It's not too bad," Mia says.

She sits on the bed and is immediately swarmed by half a dozen roaches.

"Sorry. I have some bothersome roommates."

She chuckles, brushes the roaches off. "I can deal."

Parker sits next to her.

"So," Mia says.

"So," Parker says.

They look into each other's eyes. This close, it sinks in for Parker just how *hot* she is. Her hair is silky and flowing. Her face is perfectly proportioned. Her floral dress delicately accentuates her luscious curves.

She also smells like gasoline, but the appendage

currently pitching a tent in Parker's pants seems willing to overlook that.

"Ooh, is that for me?" Mia asks, seeing the erection.

"I think, uh, we should kiss first," Parker says.

"Good idea."

She removes the gas mask, tosses it aside. They each lean forward and their lips press together. Hers taste like the coffee from earlier, but Parker does his best to ignore it. It's been a long time since he's kissed a woman, just as long since he's had sex. Not since . . . since Charlotte. He resolved after what happened to never date nor sleep with a woman again, but there's no denying how much he's missed it, how frustrated he's been. His body burns with desire.

Mia slips her dress straps over her shoulders and lets the garment fall down past her perky, round breasts. She isn't wearing a bra. Parker pulls off his shirt. She pulls the dress the rest of the way off and lays down on the pillow in nothing but her panties. He removes his shorts and underwear and slides her panties down her legs and over her feet.

But . . . wait.

"This is wrong, isn't it?" he asks.

"Why's that?"

"They can't just force you to get pregnant. It's your body."

"What can we do? Do you want to go to prison?"

"There has to be some way to resist. I don't relish the idea of bringing more children into this world."

"There's no time to figure something out. They made it very clear that we have to do this as soon as we can. I don't want to get pregnant either, but this is the United States government we're talking about. Resistance isn't an option."

"But—"

"Parker, listen. We are currently ass-naked in bed with each other. I am so goddamn fucking horny I could scream.

So could you please shut the hell up and screw me already?"

She's right; they might as well make the best of their situation. He lowers himself flat on top of her, kisses her. Flesh pressing together, they merge into a two-backed beast. She takes his cock in her hand, strokes him softly as she guides him. With a gasp, he shoves inside her.

Holy *shit*. He's forgotten how good this feels. The tight, wet warmth of her pussy puts his hand to shame. He thrusts and thrusts, grunting with exertion, with pleasure. He fucks her and fucks her and fucks her. She moans, gasps, shrieks, squeals, and squirms. She digs her long fingernails into his back and buttocks. She spreads her legs and raises her knees and pulls her feet back behind his ears.

"Oh, God," she breathes. "Harder, harder. Faster."

Parker obliges, ramming into her so hard and so deep that she screams. He pulls back, rams forward, pulls back, rams forward. As hard and fast as he can he fucks her, and she screams and screams and he fucks her and she thrashes and claws at his skin and he fucks her and he's nearly there, to orgasm, and he wraps his arms tight around her and prepares for the great gushing splurge of his seed to be unleashed in an explosion of ecstasy.

And then the person beneath him is no longer Mia, but Charlotte. Mia's face is Charlotte's face; her moans are Charlotte's moans. And Charlotte's face becomes a bloody mess of sinew and bone, her flesh half-chewed away by hungry little mandibles, and . . .

Parker screams. He pulls out, and Mia's Mia again, looking confused. Parker jumps off the bed, rushes to the bathroom and slams the door. He guzzles water from the tap and splashes it over his face.

"Parker?" Mia knocks on the door. "What happened?"

"I . . . I'm sorry. I don't know. A panic attack."

"Are you okay?"

"I will be in a moment."

More knocking, but not on the bathroom door. Someone's in the hallway. "Open up!" a man shouts. "Don't bother putting your clothes on, just get out here!"

How'd they know Parker and Mia weren't wearing clothes? Check that; the whole building must know after the racket they made. Is it someone angry about the noise?

"I'm an agent of the Department of Fertility and Population Expansion! Open this door in ten seconds or you'll be fined!"

Parker says, "I'd really rather get my clothes—"

"Ten! Nine! Eight . . ."

Parker exits the bathroom and opens the door. He holds both hands over his genitals, covering them.

A constipated-looking man in a black suit and white tie stands in the hallway. "You retreated rather suddenly from intercourse. Did something happen?"

"You were *watching?*" Parker demands.

"Naturally. Compliance must be ensured. Did you cum?"

"Where were you watching *from?*"

"Answer the question. Did you or did you not inject your semen into your partner?"

Parker's pretty sure he didn't. "Yes," he says.

"Good. You may return to your business."

The man leaves and Parker closes the door.

The agent's quick willingness to accept Parker's lie discomforts him. The email promised investigation in the event of suspected foul play. He and Mia can't really be getting off the hook this easily, can they? Maybe they've just gotten lucky. *This* time.

"I'm gonna clean up a bit and get dressed, okay?" Parker says. He returns to the bathroom, wets a washcloth and scrubs himself down with soap. Wetting the washcloth a second time, he uses it to clean his hair. He puts the washcloth down, takes a piss, dresses, and leaves the bathroom.

Mia, redressed, reclines on his bed. "Hey, honey," she

says sweetly. She pats the mattress beside her. "Gonna join me?"

Parker frowns. "Er, Mia . . . "

"Yes? Is there a problem?"

"You can't stay here."

The sudden coldness of her expression just about stops Parker's heart. Their passionate intercourse almost made him forget that she's a psychopath.

"It's—it's not that I don't *want* you to," he stammers. "It's just . . . that mattress is tiny. There's not enough room for both of us to sleep."

"You can sleep on top of me, then. Or I on top of you . . . " She smiles slyly. "The thought's already making me horny again. We could try making love a second time. Maybe you'll cum."

Make love. She's already thinking in those terms? This is bad. He has to be straight with her, even if it puts him in danger. He may find himself in even more danger later if he doesn't shut down her misconception. Next to the fridge, he spots the claw hammer he used a few days ago to fix his wooden bedframe. He edges toward it.

"I think you've got the wrong idea here," he says. "It's not just about the bed being too small. I'm really not ready for a committed relationship."

Mia sits up on the bed. She looks down so he can't see her eyes, but her tone resonates icy fury. "Are you fucking kidding me?"

Parker shuffles another step closer to the hammer, slowly, so as not to give himself away.

"I cannot believe you," she says. "I thought you were different, but I guess I was wrong."

"I was hurt. Badly," Parker says. "In a previous relationship. It doesn't have anything to do with you."

"Right now, *you're* hurting *me.* I have feelings, you know. You can't just yank me around and expect me not to—"

"Mia, be an adult about this. Aren't I allowed to say no?"

"*After* you've slept with me? I'm not some slut. I'm not a fuck toy. Why do men always think it's okay to just jump my bones and then throw me away like I don't even matter? I thought you were different from the others, but I guess I was wrong. You're *just* like them. All you want me for is sex!"

"*Jesus Christ, I don't fucking* want *you at all!*"

Mia leaps, snarling, from the bed. Parker lunges for the hammer, grabs it and holds it in front of him. "Step back."

Mercifully, she obeys. Rage doesn't leave her eyes, though. Not even a little bit. "Don't want me at all?" she repeats.

"I didn't mean it like . . . look. Here's the thing. This whole thing was arranged for us," Parker says. "I didn't get any say in it. Some guy just called me and said hey, make babies with this woman or you're going to jail. Am I going to say I didn't at least somewhat enjoy the conversations we've had, the parts when you didn't have a knife at my throat? Am I going to say I didn't enjoy the sex? No. I'd be lying if I said those things. You could use some medication and a therapist, but I don't think you're a bad person. I *have* enjoyed this. It's just, if it were up to me? I wouldn't have met you at the café. I wouldn't have had sex with you. Not because you're you, but because those things open the risk of getting attached, and I don't like to get attached. In my life, attachment leads to pain."

Mia sits back down on the bed. Again, she lowers her head, so he can't see her face.

"I understand," she says, softly.

Parker expels a long breath. Thank God.

"I understand," she says again, leaning forward. "That you . . . " She shoots off the bed, grabs the hammer faster than he can pull it away. She wrenches it from his grip and hurls it across the room, where it dents the wall and falls onto the bed. Parker shoves her back, but she makes a fist and drives her knuckles into his stomach. " . . . are a complete fucking piece of *shit!*"

Parker doubles over, gasping. Mia plants a kick to his shoulder that knocks him into the fridge. She kicks again, but he recovers, blocks, and dodges toward the bed. He dives onto the mattress, arm outstretched for the hammer. *Crack!* The bedframe breaks. The mattress goes to an angle, spilling Parker into the wall. The hammer clatters across the floor, out of reach.

Mia jumps onto the bed. Parker kicks her back, rolls to the floor, stands up. He faces her.

"There's a reason every man you've been with left you," he says. "It's because you're completely *insane*. You don't need medication and a therapist. You need to be institutionalized!"

"Don't you dare tell me I'm in—"

The apartment door bursts open and a man in a goat costume charges into the room and tackles Parker through the window. They plummet among thick glass shards sparkling in the air. A big, soft mattress cushions the landing, but it still knocks the wind from Parker.

A man with an ivy cap and walrus mustache runs over, lifts a black megaphone to his lips and bellows, "Cut, cut, *cut!* Who put that mattress there?"

Above, Mia leans out the window. "Don't you dare try to run off, you coward! I know where you live!"

"I'm not running off. I have no clue what's going on!" Parker shouts. Then, to the man with the megaphone he asks, "What's going on?"

"We're redoing the scene. Get back up there."

Past the director, Parker sees the DFPE agent attempting—and failing—to hide behind a wall as he spies on them.

"Hey!" Parker shouts. "I see you over there!"

"You don't see a thing," the agent says.

"Now I hear you, too."

"What do you want?"

"The partner you guys assigned me? She's trying to kill me."

"So?"

Parker rises off the mattress and storms over to the agent. The director calls after him, "Hey, we've got a scene to—"

"Fuck off!" Parker shouts at the director. He seizes the agent by the shoulders and pulls him out of hiding. "What do you mean, *so?*"

"Hands off. Now."

Parker lets go.

"I'm not obligated to answer your questions, but I will, since I'm a nice guy. At the DFPE our only concern is that you meet the two-child minimum requirement. Whatever else you do, or don't do, as a couple means little to us."

"Can't you pair me with someone else?"

"All partners have been carefully selected based on a variety of factors. Any other pairing will produce lower-quality offspring."

"So, I have no rights at all, here."

"Please also note that the police have been instructed not to interfere with relationships created by the DFPE."

"If you won't help, and the police won't help, then what am I supposed to do?"

"I recommend either purchasing a weapon or taking self-defense classes. I'm sorry, but there is nothing else I can do for you."

"Excuse me," the director says. "It is highly inappropriate for you to fraternize while on set. I am afraid that as of now, you are no longer part of this film."

"I never signed up to be part of your stupid film!"

The director shakes his head. "Just unbelievable." He and his crew pack their equipment and leave.

Mia exits the apartment building and approaches Parker.

Parker says, "Listen—"

"Shut up," she snaps. "I'll leave for now, but this is *not* over."

Mia walks down the street, and Parker returns to his

room. He fixes the angle of his mattress and lies down. He hurts everywhere. His stomach hurts where Mia punched him, his shoulder where she kicked him. Other parts ache from the fall. A sharper pain throbs beneath his arm, where he looks and sees crimson staining the sleeve of his shirt. He pulls it off. A laceration in his armpit leaks blood. It doesn't look deep. He can thank the safety glass for that. It's designed not to make serious cuts. Parker's lucky. If just one or two factors had been different, he'd be more than just hurting. He'd be halfway to the grave, if not in it.

But Mia will be back—and he may not be so lucky next time.

CHAPTER FOUR

THUMP.

Parker opens his eyes.

Thump. Thump.

He turns on the lamp.

Thump. Thump. Thump.

The sound is inside the wall. Or it's coming from the next room over. There's no one in that room, though. There *can't* be, because that whole section of the building is sealed off by the mold.

Thump.

Sounds too big to be mice. What else gets inside of walls? Raccoons, maybe?

Thump.

Waaaaaah!

Uh . . . all righty, then. That's a big old serving of what the fuck. Was that a baby? It was, no mistaking it. A baby, inside his wall.

Waaaaaaaaah!

Parker gets the hammer. Goes to his hands and knees on the floor and turns the head toward the wall. He hopes he doesn't hit the kid, but what's he supposed to do? He's got to get it out of there somehow. He swings, and the hammer penetrates the plaster. Swings some more until he's made a hole big enough to look through. There's a hollow corridor about a foot wide inside the wall where something small could fit. As he looks, a tiny head passes the hole, then pink pajamas on a tiny body. Parker reaches in and makes a grab for the infant's foot, hoping to keep it in place while he works on the wall, but misses, fingers just brushing the toes as they move out of reach.

He resumes his impromptu carpentry project. It takes a while, and his arms ache by the time he's done, but eventually he's made a hole big enough to pull the baby out. When it passes again, he takes it by the torso and hauls it through the hole.

He knows this kid. He doesn't know her name, but he's seen her from time to time with the Cromwells who live down the hall. Standing, careful not to drop her, he unlocks and opens the door and walks across the mold carpet to their apartment. He knocks.

No answer, but Parker hears more crying inside. He knocks again. Waits. Tries several more times.

The Cromwells aren't home. Parker sighs. Like it or not, he's on babysitting duty tonight. He takes the girl back to his room, shuts and locks the door. Now, there's the question of where she'll sleep. The bed's no good, she might fall off it. Or he might accidentally roll over her in his sleep.

An idea sparks. Parker places the girl on the bed, turns to the kitchen counter and pulls open a drawer. It's wide, long, and deep enough to fit a baby. He takes it all the way out and dumps the contents, mostly miscellaneous kitchen utensils, onto the counter. Then, he sets it down on the floor. He goes to the bathroom, pulls two towels off the rack and returns. He lays one towel over the bottom of the drawer and puts the girl on top. The other towel he puts over her, like a blanket. It's not a crib, but it's the best he can do.

Before he goes to bed himself, Parker checks the room to make sure there's nothing hazardous on the floor. Determining it to be safe, he lays down. He closes his eyes and soon, sleep begins to take over.

And the girl starts to cry again.

In the morning, Parker returns to the Cromwells'. Mr. Cromwell opens the door after a moment. By the looks of it, he's just climbed out of bed. His brown hair's an uncombed mess, his shirt's on backwards, and his fly is down.

He rubs his eyes, yawns and says, "What are you doing pounding on my door before I've had a chance to drink my morning coffee?" Only then does his gaze fall to the girl in Parker's arms, and his eyes narrow. "Did you kidnap my daughter? That's not cool."

"Obviously I didn't kidnap her, since I'm bringing her back," Parker says. "I found her crawling around inside the wall last night. I knocked on your door, but you didn't seem to be home so I let her sleep at my place."

Mr. Cromwell yawns again, and Parker yawns, too. The child allowed him sleep only in fits and starts.

"Sorry about that," Mr. Cromwell says. "Anita and I stayed late at a friend's house."

"And you left your kids alone?"

"Well, it's not like we can afford a babysitter."

"That doesn't make it okay."

"'Doesn't make it okay?' Who are you, the morality police? They're not your kids. You don't get to tell us what is or isn't *okay* about how we raise them."

Parker gives an exasperated throw of his hands. "They're way too young to take care of themselves! If you're gone and they get hungry, or they hurt themselves, what are they supposed to do?"

"Tough it out. It'll make them stronger when they grow up." Mr. Cromwell flexes his biceps. "Strong like me."

"And if they can't manage to 'tough it out?' If one or more of them dies due to your neglect, what then?"

"If they die, they die. In nature, infants die all the time. It doesn't matter as long as the females of a species bear enough children to offset the losses. So, even if we lose a few, we're still doing our part to grow the population. Besides, we can make more."

"What are you talking about? We aren't *in* nature!"

"We're not?" Mr. Cromwell gestures to the mold on the walls. "I beg to differ."

Parker's route to the subway station takes him past an elementary school, an austere, three-story brick building surrounded by chain-link fencing. Class begins soon, and the road out front is clogged with buses and vehicles of parents dropping off their kids.

Across the street from the school, a crowd of protestors have gathered at the mouth of an alleyway. In unison, they chant, "No sex ed! Mrs. Johnson is a shithead! No sex ed! Mrs. Johnson is a shithead!"

Some of them hold signs. One shows a pack of Trojan condoms in a red circle with a line running through. Another says, "What good is English, history, or math? Teach copulation, not calculation!"

"Hey!" a woman calls to Parker. "Can we get a moment of your time?"

"No, thanks," Parker says, but she steps in front of him, blocking his way.

"Do you think Mrs. Johnson is a shithead?" she asks.

"Why's she a shithead?" Parker asks.

"Because she's teaching our kids about *safe sex*."

"Uh . . . " Parker scratches his head. "That's controversial now?"

"Don't be stupid. We are facing an existential emergency. It may have been acceptable to teach kids about condoms and other such things in the past, but times have changed. We need to be doing everything we can to get our numbers up in the wake of this horrible decline. And she's in there trying to *diminish* teen pregnancy rates?

That bitch, she doesn't even have any kids of her own. Talk about setting a terrible example!"

Before today, Parker would've been content to carry on and leave this woman to her madness. The particular hysteria she's spouting, however, is exactly what's at the root of Parker's current circumstances.

"Please, enlighten me," Parker says. "What is just *so bad* about a fraction of a percentage drop in population that it warrants what you and so many others demand?"

"Fewer workers," she says.

"Capitalist propaganda, how predictable," Parker says. "Poor corporations, struggling so desperately to fill jobs they're not even offering. Besides, what about immigrants?"

"Razor wire, landmines—"

"There are two primary means to replenish a country's depleting population, and consequently, its workforce. The first is for citizens to have more children. The second is to allow people in from the outside. Doesn't it seem like we should be doing more to embrace immigration before turning to measures such as the Population Expansion Act, or pushing teenagers to have more unsafe sex?"

"You're talking about pissing in our gene pool by inviting in a bunch of *Spics*."

"Well, aren't you a walking stereotype," Parker says. "Let me hear another reason about why all this fear-mongering is justified."

"The elder care crisis. The average age on Earth is increasing and there are fewer young people to take care of all the old people."

Props to her, she's actually managed to produce a cogent point. This one hits home for Parker, as he thinks of poor Mrs. Plymouth left to wither uncared for, forgotten by the world. She's far from the only senior citizen confined to that fate. This problem has existed for many years now, and it's only been getting worse. However, while "more children" is the most obvious solution to the issue, Parker doesn't think it's the right one. People are people, not tools to solve the problems of those that came before them. A parent who has a child only for the benefits it will bring that parent as they age has given no more thought to the creation of a sentient being than to the purchase of a screwdriver.

Parker voices some of his thoughts. The woman goes silent for a minute, then says, "So, you hate old people?"

"That's it," Parker says, walking away. "Start bringing out straw men like that and I'm done with this conversation."

"Hey, come back here!" she shouts. "You can't advocate for genocide of the elderly and then just walk away!"

Parker keeps walking. The woman grabs his arm and starts to say something, but is cut off by a flurry of enraged shouting as a man rushes toward them, wearing something strapped to his chest.

"Child haters!" the man roars. "Communist Nazis, proponents of decline! Trying to fuck us all by teaching our kids about birth control! Why don't *you* get fucked instead!"

Parker screams, realizing what the object is on the man's chest.

A bomb.

Parker sprints off down the alley as the man tears by, toward the student-packed buses. The alley turns a corner and Parker takes it, putting a building between himself and the blast. He ducks down and covers his ears.

Boom.

The explosion shakes the ground and shatters windows, sending glass tinkling into the alley. Parker stands and uncovers his ears to a cacophony of screaming, crying, and car alarms. Smoke pours into the sky over the alleyway.

The woman he'd been arguing with storms around the corner. The blast has made a gory shambles of the right half of her face.

"I told you I still have more to say," she says. "You know if decline con . . . continues at the . . . "

She collapses face-first on the ground.

Outside the alley, children continue to scream.

At the subway station, a man watches a program on his phone at full volume. Parker glances at the man's screen. It's a talk show. Parker's not familiar with the host or his guest.

"Tell me a little bit about these views of yours that have been garnering so much attention lately," the host says.

"Well, it's no secret that the number of humans on this planet is diminishing rapidly," the guest says. "We're facing an unprecedented crisis as a species. The only way to avoid complete and total societal collapse is to get total fertility levels back above the replacement rate of two-point-one children per woman. And to put it frankly, the clock is ticking. I'm glad Congress and the president are finally taking some much-needed action here with the new Population Expansion Act, but it's not even close to enough. We mustn't stop at requiring women to have only two children."

"If not two, what number do you think we should be striving for?"

"Simply put? The *maximum possible*. As in, a fertile woman must give birth every nine months for as long as she is capable. With assisted reproductive technology, we can see to it that she never gives birth to any less than two children at a time, though ten or more is optimal. Remember that Iowa woman who was on the news a few years back, who got her body modified to give birth to, uh, twenty children at once? Vigintuplets, I think was the word. Imagine every fertile woman in America giving birth to vigintuplets every nine months. That's where we need to be. Furthermore, I'm not just talking about *women,* as in, adults. What I'm saying here should apply to *all fertile females,* period. Over the last few decades, girls have been hitting puberty at earlier ages. There've been an increasing number of reports of girls experiencing menarche as young as two, three, in some cases less than a year old. We need to be impregnating these young girls as soon as their bodies can viably carry a pregnancy to term. And then we need to *keep* impregnating them until it is no longer biologically possible for them to conceive."

"What about the complications that arise from pregnancy at that age? The strain on the heart? The fact the developing body is deprived of critical nutrients, such as calcium, as they're diverted to the fetus? Higher risk of preeclampsia? Those are just a few of many examples. The mortality rate is far higher among young girls than it is among adult women."

"Those are the necessary costs of saving humanity."

"It sounds like you don't care much about women's rights in all of this. They're just breeding machines to you?"

"Fuck you. *Fuck* you. You think I came onto your show to be attacked and disrespected? I love women. I have a wife. I have eighteen daughters. How dare you say I want women to be treated like machines. I'm not proposing that they not be allowed to live their lives the way they want, outside of procreation and raising the children by themselves. I'm not proposing they have all their rights and free will taken away from them. Each and every one of us has an obligation to do what's best for the human species. This is about fulfilling that obligation. Every woman, doing her part. That's all."

"What about the workforce?"

"What about it?"

"You have eighteen daughters. You must understand how much time it takes to raise that many children. But you're suggesting each woman should have even more children than that. There's no conceivable way she can care for all of them and still have time to go to work. You'd be effectively eliminating half the workforce."

"There's 'no conceivable way?' My wife does it. She takes care of the children and she works forty hours a week. *And* she makes dinner every night for all of us. You know how she does it? She's got this thing, maybe you've heard about it—in a history book, probably, since the concept's gone the way of the dinosaur in our modern society—it's called a *work ethic*."

"Let me get this straight. You say you want every woman to work forty hours a week, raise dozens of children, and cook dinner for the whole family every single night? And you also claim to care about women being allowed and having the time to do what they want?"

"Fuck you. I don't have to take this from you. This interview is over."

Parker arrives five minutes late to work. The Dwight-thing is still there near the break room, still screaming.

Natasha looks up from her cubicle.

"Not in the mood, Natasha," Parker says. "I just bore witness to yet another horrific tragedy that will haunt me for the rest of my life. No problem, it's only like, the third time in a week."

Uncharacteristically, Natasha doesn't answer. That's when Parker notices the maroon splotches around her right eye.

"What happened?" he asks.

"It's the partner they assigned me. He's a piece of shit."

"Let me guess. You reached out and asked the Department of Fertility and Population Expansion if they could assign you someone different, but they insisted that no other partnership would produce the same quality offspring."

"Yeah."

"We're in the same boat."

Natasha eyes Parker curiously, as if noticing for the

first time that he's a person. He, too, feels an unprecedented spark of connection. They've been at each other's throats since that sandwich incident, but now, they're going through the exact same thing.

"I'm sorry," Natasha says.

"Thanks. Sorry it's happening to you, too."

"An ex of mine used to do these kinds of things to me," Natasha says. "I escaped from him. I told myself, never again. And yet...here we are."

Parker wants to say something, but the phone rings. He answers with the usual phrase.

"Pickled Klingons in heat," the caller says.

"Brush your teeth with extra soap," Parker says, and hangs up.

He glares at the phone, willing it not to ring again, *ever* again. Because fuck this job. The government is forcing people into abusive relationships with no means of escape, and he's here doing...what? What *is* this job? Who are the callers? Does any of this even *mean* anything? What can be so important about answering a phone and saying, "Brush your teeth with extra soap?" It's hogwash. Capital-B Bullshit.

But this is where the money comes from, and money equals food and a bed, so he answers the phone and says his gibberish, hangs up and does it again, ad nauseam. Across from him Natasha does the same, equally trapped as he is. They should be out there *doing* something, anything, to fix this. Instead? May Jesus lactate in your anus. Bioluminescent cheesefuck surprise.

That right there sums up Parker's life. All of it, nothing but nonsense.

After work, Natasha asks to meet with Parker in the empty box room at the top of the ladder. He clocks out and joins her there. She skittishly looks around as if she thinks someone might be hiding among the stacks, eavesdropping.

Satisfied no one's there but them, she says, "We need to put our feud behind us."

"I agree," Parker says. "It's childish."

"Whoa, whoa. No. I've had a perfectly valid reason to dislike you. You *ate my special mustard.*"

"Which I've apologized for many times—"

"You couldn't just fucking *ask* whose sandwich was whose? Was that too much of an *inconvenience* for you?"

"It was a mistake! And you *just* said you wanted to drop it!"

"Yes, until you called me childish!"

"Okay. You're right. I apologize for that, too. Are we good?"

"Good enough. I'm only doing this because we're both in a similar bind right now. I think we can help each other out."

"How so?"

Natasha roundhouse kicks a box, sending it and the rest of its stack tumbling to the floor.

"Why'd you do that?" Parker asks.

"Thought someone might be hiding there."

"You're being paranoid."

"Can't be too paranoid. Anyway, here's what I'm thinking. That fuckhead won't beat me if I've got someone else around for backup."

"So, you're asking me? What about someone you *don't* hate for a minor incident involving a sandwich?"

"It wasn't a minor—I mean, no. I . . . " She slumps. "I don't really know anyone."

That's news to Parker. He'd always assumed Natasha had friends. She's outgoing enough, but you can never know what's going on beneath a person's surface.

"Hey, guys!" Janice pops her head up from the top of the ladder. "What's going on?"

"Shit!" Natasha says. "I thought you left already!"

"Why can't Janice hear this?" Parker asks.

"Yeah, come on," Janice says. "I've been affected, too. My husband's in jail because of it."

Parker didn't know Janice had a husband. He's learning a lot about his coworkers today. "What happened?"

"They told us we're not allowed to have sex with each other anymore, only with the partners they've assigned. We did it anyway, but then an agent came by and told us they'd been spying on our intimacy and they would punish us if they caught us again. Eli got livid. He flew at that agent guy who came to reprimand us, just jumped on him, started pummeling him in the face. After that, the police came and carted him away. I haven't even been allowed to talk to him since then."

"That's terrible," Parker says. "Okay." He turns to Natasha. "Natasha, I'll go with you when you meet your partner if you'll do the same for me. Janice, I don't know what we can do about your husband, but maybe we'll think of something."

"Plan sounds good to me," Natasha says.

Janice nods in agreement.

Together, the three of them navigate the ventilation maze and head down the stairs.

"I need to go," Janice says once they reach the first floor. "Let's trade phone numbers."

"Mine is 555-476-7912," Parker says.

Natasha and Janice enter it into their phones. Parker's phone dings twice—messages from each of them, with their own numbers.

To Natasha, Janice says, "My number is—"

The entry door and wall around it blows apart as Mia's enlarged face crashes into the building. Janice has only time to unleash the beginning of a scream before several speeding tons of steel slam her into the wall.

CHAPTER FIVE

MIA REVERSES revealing the damage. The sheer force of the impact has embedded Janice's pulverized remains into the wood. The twisted, blood-leaking horror among the jagged splinters is so thoroughly crushed and mangled it doesn't resemble a person. Parker represses the urge to vomit.

Mia turns her front wheels so her cab, her face, faces Parker.

"You killed her!" Parker screams. "You're a murderer!"

"Cheaters must be taught a *lesson,*" Mia says coldly.

"Cheater? What in the hell are you talking about? And how did you know where I work?"

Behind Mia, Natasha slips quietly onto the stairs. Parker focuses his eyes on Mia so she won't wonder what he's looking at back there, won't turn around to see.

"I installed a tracking app on your phone while you were in the bathroom last night," Mia says.

"That's fucked up."

"The app also records sound. I've heard every word you've said to these two women. You're planning to get rid of me so you can be with one of them instead. Which do you lust after most? The one I just killed? Or the other?"

"That's a rather radical interpretation of the conversation I had with them."

"I know that hussy just went up the stairs. It doesn't matter if she runs. I'll catch her. I'll ensure you'll have no one left but me."

At the back of the hall, someone shouts, *"Shit!"*, followed by an explosion at Mia's rear.

Mia shrieks, "Did someone just shoot a missile at my *ass?*"

For once, Parker's glad for the existence of Bildo's Dildos. Their accidental missile firing provides the distraction he needs to dash past Mia and up the stairs.

"Get back here!" Mia shouts. She can't follow him as she is now, but Parker has no idea how long it takes her to transform back to human form. Minutes? Seconds? She could be right on his heels.

He turns onto the fourth floor. The hall ends with an exit that leads out to a fire escape. Parker could go that way, but then he'd be leaving Natasha behind. She's probably gone to their workplace because it's the part of the building she's most familiar with. He ducks into the vent and sure enough, someone's wiped the arrows away to smudges, obfuscating the way forward.

Parker follows his memory about which way to turn at each juncture. Fortunately, he's done this hundreds of times and he soon reaches the empty box room. He climbs down the ladder and enters their workplace. The lights are on and the door to Vic's office is open. From the sound of it, someone's rummaging around inside.

It's Natasha. She's turned the whole room inside out, searching for something. She sits on Vic's office chair, his laptop in her lap.

"I can't believe she's dead," Natasha says. "Janice never did anything bad to anyone."

Parker only nods. "That's my partner, Mia. I knew she was crazy, but I never thought she'd . . . "

"I'm gonna fucking kill her."

"That won't be easy. You saw what she can do."

"I'll find a way. Just need to get out of here first."

"Is that what you're looking for in here? A way out?"

"Yeah. The normal way out, through the vents, is extremely impractical in case of an emergency. I figure Vic's likely got a secret exit for use in such occasions."

She types out a phrase on the laptop's keyboard and hits enter. A message appears, "Incorrect password."

"Damn." She shakes her head. "It can't be that complex. Vic's an idiot. You got any ideas? I already tried 'password' and all variations thereof."

"Uh . . . 12345?"

"Tried all the linear number sequences up to ending with nine. Didn't work." She types another phrase. The screen changes to a desktop. "Yes! Got it."

"What'd you put in?"

"Huge penis, but with 3's instead of e's and a 1 instead of an i. Now . . . "

"What are you hoping to find on there?"

"Something just like this."

She clicks an icon on the desktop. The icon's labeled, "Open Secret Door." A section of the back wall slides open, revealing an unlit passage.

"After you," Natasha says.

Parker turns on his phone's flashlight, revealing a narrow hallway full of cobwebs and carpeted in a layer of dust. An elevator sits at the far end.

Parker enters, Natasha close behind. He brushes aside the cobwebs with his hands to keep them from getting them in his face. Halfway to the elevator, a crack sounds beneath his feet.

"What was that?" Natasha asks.

"Nothing good. Keep going," Parker says.

Parker takes another step and suddenly he's sinking, the floorboards giving way beneath his weight. He tries to leap to safer ground, but his right leg slips, drops, and the rest of him follows, tumbling down into deeper darkness. He hits the floor below with a heavy thud and there's a second thud as Natasha lands beside him.

"Shit," she says.

"Are you hurt?" Parker asks.

"No."

Neither is he. They didn't fall far. He shines his light at the hole above them—

He blinks. There is no hole above them.

"Hey, you remember falling through that floor just now, right?" he says.

"Sure do."

"So where's the hole?"

"Gone, along with my sanity, probably, and our prospects of getting out of here."

"There's gotta be some way out."

"I'm not saying I'm giving up. I'm just pretty sure that, right now, this building wants to kill us."

Parker stands up, dusts himself off. He shines the light around. They're in another hallway, a bigger one, with five doors on each side and one at either end.

"Pick a door, any door," Parker mutters.

He tries the one closest. Locked. Natasha tries another—also locked. The third door opens, but leads only to yet another hallway. A second hallway branches off to the side, access blocked by a set of vertical metal bars.

"Why would someone put bars here?" Parker asks.

"I always knew something was wrong with this building," Natasha says.

They try a few more doors until they find another that opens. A downward staircase greets them on the other side.

"Down is good," Parker says. Down means they're getting closer to the first floor.

So, down they go. At the bottom of the stairs, they find another door. It opens upon—big surprise—another hallway. On their left, more doors; to the right, a set of bars nearly identical to those on the floor above.

Or, wait . . . no. It can't be.

Beyond the bars stands an open door, and beyond that, a staircase leading down. They're not nearly identical— they're the same goddamn bars.

Natasha shakes her head and says, "Fuck."

Parker concurs.

"Which door now?" he asks.

"Does it matter?"

"It has to."

The first door he tries groans open. Here's a change of scenery, not a hallway or stairs but a room, and Parker's hope soars because there are people here, and they must know the way out. Each person sits at a cubicle like the one he has grown so intimately familiar with, but instead of phones there are computer monitors, bulky ones like Parker has seen in pictures from the eighties and nineties. Every screen shows the same thing, a flickering, black-and-white blur of static.

"Excuse me," Parker says.

No answer.

"Something's wrong with them," Natasha whispers.

Parker steps in for a closer look. The people sit unmoving. A row of gaunt faces stare unblinking at the digital blizzards in front of them. Parker waves his hand in front of a woman's face, gets no response. Dead inside.

Something creaks in the back of the room and Parker's heart does a full stop like someone's slammed on the brakes. Next to him, Natasha stares wide-eyed in the direction of the sound.

Nothing happens.

"Old building," Parker says with a nervous laugh. "Bound to make some creepy noises."

Natasha visibly relaxes as well. "Let's get out of this room," she says. "I don't—"

An anemic hand shoots out from under the table and seizes Natasha by the ankle. She screams. Behind the hand, in the dark, yellow eyes glow over a nose and mouth masked in blue cloth. A man crawls forward, letting go of Natasha in order to rise to a standing position. He's easily more than seven feet tall, clad in a white doctor's coat.

Natasha flees the room. Parker stays rooted to the spot, part deer-in-the-headlights effect, part curiosity. "Who are you?" he asks.

"Call me Dr. Shellick."

"You're the orthodontist from downstairs? What are you doing here?"

"I'm just here to treat my patient."

"I'm not your patient."

"That's why your teeth are no good. I know you used to wear braces as a child, but you couldn't stop picking apart the wires. I know you switched to wearing a retainer instead but it made you feel uncomfortable so you gave up and never tried again. We're going to rectify that mistake."

Now Parker flees, because Dr. Shellick knows way too much about him, and he may not know much about the man's treatment methods, but he knows what they sound like.

"Running won't fix your teeth!" Shellick shouts.

Parker dashes down the hall. "Natasha?" he calls. "Where are you?"

"Over here!"

From behind a door on Parker's right. He opens the door. On the other side, yet another hallway. No—the same hallway. Screw this shit. "Natasha!"

"Here!" She sounds much farther away than before. Her voice echoes as though they're in a canyon, *here, here, here, here . . .*

Dr. Shellick lumbers into the hallway toting a large, orange case in one hand. Parker has no clue where the case came from, since Shellick didn't have it a moment ago, but he instantly knows what's in it from the shape. Rectangular, with a long, rounded protrusion. Dr. Shellick sets it down, clicks open the latches. He hoists the chainsaw in the air. Parker imagines a psychopathic grin beneath that mask.

"Let's fix those teeth," Shellick says.

The chainsaw revs to life. Shellick takes a step forward. Parker tries a door, locked. Shellick's a step closer, another step, saw's teeth spinning, spinning, spinning. Parker backs away. His shaking hands fumble at one knob after another, always met with the same terrible obstinance.

Until there's only one door left, behind him. He takes the knob—it turns!

He throws open the door, but behind it is another door, smaller. Behind that door's another door, and behind that another. The chainsaw roars loud in Parker's ears. He frantically works through the ridiculous recursion of doors, certain that at any second, the chainsaw will sink into him and his soft flesh will be ripped through like butter by that savage, whirling dance of metal teeth.

The last door is half Parker's height and it opens to a ceilinged passage. He ducks inside and runs through at a crouch, bursting out the other end into a roomful of hook-hung pig carcasses. In the warmth of the room, the carcasses have spoiled. Their rancid stench forces Parker's fingers to his nose. He pushes into the mucid cluster of hanging rot, searching for another exit.

"You surely don't want to *keep* your teeth like that, do you?" Shellick asks, and his voice seems to come from everywhere in the room.

Parker can't be sure in the meager light of his phone's flashlight, but he thinks he sees one of the carcasses move. He shakes his head, certain he's imagined it—then it moves again. With a loud snap, the carcass drops to the floor. It lifts its head, and it's no normal pig but a large, twisted mutation of one, with long, flaccid penises dangling from its jowls and snout. The creature lumbers forward, and the movement spurs the penises to spurt cum onto the floor.

Parker backs away, into another hanging carcass. A long slit opens on the pig-thing's back and something that looks like a three-headed human baby climbs out, covered in fluid. The Cerberus baby leaps onto Parker, causing him to drop his phone. It lands, flashlight facing down, on the floor, plunging the room into stygian blackness. Parker wrestles with the baby in the dark and successfully manages to throw it off him. He stoops, feeling on the ground for his phone, but the pig-thing bowls into him, knocking him back. He leaves the phone and scurries away, pushing past pig carcasses.

"Why yes, I believe I will have ham for dinner," Shellick says, and the chainsaw starts up again. The pig-thing squeals as the saw tears it to shreds.

Parker sees a dim light shining and moves towards it. The light expands to illuminate a large, empty chamber—Shellick and the pigs are gone. In the center of the chamber stands a woman.

It's Parker's first love, his only love.

Charlotte.

"Charlotte!" he calls.

She runs away.

He knows she's not real, can't be real, but chases her anyway. The floor becomes a giant treadmill that pushes him back, as she draws farther and farther away.

"You'll never catch her like *that!*" a man shouts. "Don't be lazy, run faster!"

It's Coach Witner from high school, or at least his voice—he's a giant head of cauliflower in a tracksuit now.

"Run faster or I'll beat the fuck out of you!" Witner bellows.

"Screw off," Parker pants, wishing he'd had the guts to tell off the real Witner the same way.

The treadmill stops. Parker reaches Charlotte, but he's too late. She's been desecrated, torn apart. Oversized spiders skitter away from her corpse.

"You gonna eat that, honey?" That's Parker's mom's voice. She appears in front of him, huge and naked, and spreads apart her labia. A wave of menstrual fluid gushes out. An otter on a small surfboard hits Parker in the head and knocks him down into the fluid. He comes up a second later gasping and sputtering, soaked in his mother's menorrhea.

Her vagina sucks him in like a reverse birth, through its moist, fleshy lips and into his college dorm room.

"Enough of this Alice in Fucked-up-land crap!" Parker bellows. He's completely dry now.

"It's all *symbolism,* man," says his stoned roommate, Gary, reclined on his bed. "Metaphors and allegories and shit. *Deep* stuff."

"I can see that with Charlotte and the treadmill, maybe," Parker says. "But the otters? My freaking *mom?* Come on. It's all nonsense."

"Yeah, you're probably right," Gary says, taking a hit of pot. "Wanna hear a funny story about butts?"

"No."

"Your loss."

Gary and the room vanish, returning Parker to darkness.

"Parker?"

Parker shrieks.

"It's just me. Natasha."

Is it really her, or more of . . . whatever the hell all that was? Chemicals in the building messing with his head? If he keeps questioning like that, though, he won't be able to trust anything. He'll go forward on the assumption that she's real, for now.

"Thought I'd lost you," he says.

"Same. Did I hear a chainsaw?"

"It's that psycho Dr. Shellick."

"Well, I've got good news. There's an exit over here."

He stands. Natasha takes his hand and guides him through the pitch black.

"Don't you have a phone with a flashlight?" he asks.

"Exit's just over here," she says. Something's strange about her voice, like she's got a frog in her throat.

"What happened to your voice?" he asks.

"Exit's just over here."

He lets go of her, a chill running through him. This isn't right.

A light flares on, sudden and bright. Parker shields his eyes with his arm and blinks away spots from his vision.

And turns to run—only to find Dr. Shellick blocking the door.

"Enough games," Shellick says.

"H—how did you make yourself sound like her?" Parker asks.

Shellick gestures behind Parker, toward a dentist's chair. A spotlight shines upon the chair from some unseen source above.

Parker punches Shellick in the face and pulls back his hand with a wince. Shellick, whose face is way harder than a person's should be, doesn't even flinch.

"*Sit,*" Shellick says.

"Screw you," Parker says, failing to keep his pants-shitting terror from his voice. Then he adds, because it sounds kinda badass, "Death's not on my agenda today."

Shellick shoves Parker into the chair. Parker scrambles to get back up, but Shellick holds him down.

That wasn't badass, what Parker said. It was lame and made no sense. When is death ever on *any*one's agenda? Unless they're planning to kill themselves, nobody wakes up and thinks, *here it is; this is my day to go*. Parker didn't think that. But here he was.

Jesus, what a goddamn fucking *stupid* way to go, too. Literally getting his "teeth fixed" to death. He always hated the orthodontist as a kid, but *this* is ridiculous.

Shellick reaches into his own mouth. His hand disappears down the back of his throat and comes back with a brown, wriggling worm-thing gripped tightly in his fist. Shellick continues to pull and the thing keeps on coming. It's like a more disgusting version of that magician's trick with a length of cloth. Shellick pulls some more. There's gotta be at least four feet of the thing all coiled up on the floor like a ropy mound of shit. Five feet now. Six. Shellick stops pulling. It's all the way out.

"Ready?" Shellick asks.

"I'm leaving you a bad review on Google," Parker says. Still trying and failing to be tough because he's still not all the way connected to the reality, is still thinking there's some chance this is like that scene in every action movie where the hero's tied up, written off as dead, but finds some way to turn the tables anyhow. Deep down, Parker knows this isn't going to happen. It's just not all the way sinking in. It will, though.

Right—

About—

Shellick lifts the worm abomination's head—or anus, hard to tell which—to Parker's face.

Now.

Parker screams, because there's nothing left to do. He screams and Shellick laughs. Parker screams louder than he knew his lungs were capable of. Screams so loud it sounds not like a scream at all, but like the big, bellowing horn of some monstrous vehicle.

Wait. That isn't him.

Mia crashes into the room, splattering Shellick like a bug across her grille. She stops just short of hitting Parker.

"I can't believe you," she snarls. "You run away from me, just to come and get your fucking *teeth* cleaned?"

"He's—was—an orthodontist, not a dentist," Parker says. "And I didn't exactly volunteer."

"You're done running away. You are going to come with me and be my boyfriend now, am I clear?"

Parker disagrees. He is not, in fact, done running away. Mia can't turn or accelerate quickly as a truck, and she has no hands. In this tight space, it will be easier to run from her than Shellick.

He leaps off the chair. Mia gives a frustrated groan. He goes around the front of her and is relieved to see she's not fully blocking the door. He runs for it.

And trips.

He catches himself with one arm, sending a jolt of pain through his wrist. But it's nothing like what follows as Mia reverses and her tire runs over his foot.

Agony. Mother fuck-fuck-fuckedy-fuckin' agony.

He understands now what it means to say a pain is blinding. It obscures everything but itself. There is no world, there is no Mia, there is only the pain, an ocean of pain in which he's drowning, and he screams, and screams, and screams.

A light shines ahead. The pain's so great that Parker's dying, and here's the light of heaven come to take him. In his delirium, he reaches for it and waits for it to grow, to engulf him and whisk him away.

The light doesn't grow. It isn't the light of heaven. In her rampaging, Mia put a hole in the side of the building. That's sunlight beaming through.

Parker drags himself forward on his elbows. It takes a great mental effort to keep focused on the light ahead and not the pain in his foot. It's not that far, he tells himself. That's a lie—it might as well be millions of miles away.

Mia, reverted to her human form, puts a hand on Parker's back. "Look at you," she says. "This is pathetic, sweetheart. Being with me can't be worse than what you're doing to yourself now. Just relax and let me help you with this wound."

"Forget it," Parker hisses through gritted teeth. "You'll just run over my other foot next. Cripple me so I can't get away from you, like Annie Wilkes." He kicks out at her with his good foot.

She catches it. "If you won't have me, I'll self-destruct. I'll kill us both. I don't want to be alive if it means I can't be with you."

"You can do that?"

"I can. I really suggest you just stop strug—"

A ceiling panel falls on her head.

"Just—"

Another wallops her.

"Stop that!" she shouts at the building.

And then falls through the floor.

Parker continues dragging himself. Panels and other debris rain down around him like it's the apocalypse. Mia, in her rampaging, did so much damage to the building that it's now falling apart. Parker quickens his pace. The pain in his foot's still there, still howling at him, but he doesn't let it stop him. That opening's close, just ten feet, now nine, six, three, and then Parker slides into the light on his belly, never so happy to see the city's grimy teeming streets or breathe in its sickening smog.

He's three stories off the ground, but it doesn't matter. A huge mound of trash bags lies beneath him. He rolls over the ledge and plummets into garbage's soft, smelly embrace. Now that he's in a safe position, he's aware of just how light-headed he's become—the blood loss is doing a number on him. He lifts his head and looks down at his leg.

Some bloody, frightful mess of a thing hangs limply off the end, where his foot should be. Oh, sure, the atrocity has all the *pieces* of his foot, the metatarsals, the cuneiforms and so on, but it isn't his foot. Not anymore.

The light-headedness is quite profound now, lucidity slipping from his grasp like a slimy wet fish. Here it is, even more a certainty than before: He is dying. Perishing in the trash, of all places. How long before they find his body here? Doubtful it will be soon, the way this city operates. He'll have decomposed by then, become trash himself. Still, for all its ugliness it's a better end than that which he nearly faced by Shellick's hand. He's not restrained here. He escaped; he gets to die free.

He looks up at the smog, the great amber enigma blocking out the sky. He's not thought about it before, but that color is fitting. Amber, a preserving agent: Dead things immured within appear as if alive. He's thought of this world as dying, but that's wrong. It's dead already; it just doesn't know it.

And then, without fanfare or ceremony, with only trash around him and a city that is dead and rotting, his eyes close, and he slips quietly into the dark beyond.

The dark beyond isn't so dark. "Dimly lit" would be a better descriptor. Nor is it any kind of "beyond."

Nope, this is the same grungy planet Earth Parker thought he just left, though a different part of it. He lies not in garbage, but upon a table. A red table runner's folded and placed at the table's edge beside a stack of placemats. This is someone's dining room.

Which means Parker's gone from trash to dinner. That's at least somewhat of an improvement.

A man in a white coat enters, wearing a surgical mask. Parker panics, thinking of Shellick, before remembering that Shellick is dead.

"You're not supposed to be awake yet," the man says. "I must've done the dosing wrong again."

A doctor. That explains how Parker's still alive, and also why his foot doesn't hurt as much as before. It hurts like hell, make no mistake; just, one of the nicer circles of Hell, like the first or second rather than the eighth or ninth. He lifts his head, looks down. There's only a stump there now.

"How . . . " Parker groans. "Am I here?"

The doctor holds up a finger, indicating for Parker to wait. He lowers his mask, picks up the last bite of a sandwich off a plate, and eats it. Crumbs rain onto Parker's stump.

"Hey, I don't think that's sanitary—"

"Your friend brought you," the doctor says, wiping his lips.

"Friend?" Parker wasn't aware he had any of those.

The doctor points to the side of the room. Natasha's there, seated in a chair. She gives him a wave. "Hey there, sleepyhead. Finally up, I see."

"Natasha . . . I thought you . . . "

"Died? Almost. I thought *you* had died, until I walked past that giant pile of trash and picked up your scent."

His scent? What kind of nose did she have to pick up his scent over the far more powerful stench of all that trash?

"Thank you," he says.

"No problem."

She picks something up from her lap. It's a sandwich, wrapped in paper. She takes a bite and winces. "Hey, the fuck? This isn't my special mustard." She glares at the doctor. "You! You ate my sandwich!"

"Did I? I'm sorry. They looked so much alike."

"Screw you! Now I have nothing left to eat of it but the crumbs, and maybe I can hope there's just a little bit of mustard that fell out, too!"

The crumbs? But the crumbs are—

Natasha walks over and begins to lick the crumbs from Parker's stump.

"Come on, hurry up and finish that," the doctor says. "My family will be home soon."

Parker can't hold in his disgust. "Hey, stop! Get your tongue away from—"

"Applying additional sedative," the doctor says.

Parker passes out.

He wakes sometime later on the same table.

"All done," the doctor says. "Take a look."

Parker looks. There's no longer a stump at the bottom of his leg. Instead, there's what looks a whole lot like a small metal statue of a duck.

"Why is there a duck on my leg?" he asks.

"It's what I had on hand," the doctor says. "Gotta replace your foot with *some*thing."

"I'd rather have the stump!"

"You don't sound very grateful."

"What kind of doctor *are* you?"

"The one you could get. You'd have never gotten to the hospital in time, and even if you somehow did, you would've had to wait a long time to be seen. They're full up treating victims from that school bombing this morning."

"Thank you," Parker says. "I shouldn't be ungrateful. You saved my life. I just think the duck statue's gonna be awkward."

"Well, I could remove it, but that'd take time that I don't have right now. So, we're done here. Both of you, get lost."

"Do I get some crutches, or . . . "

"By the door."

Parker climbs off the table and immediately falls over, from a combination of missing a foot and the fact the sedative hasn't worn all the way off, making him feel like he's drunk. He looks to the doctor expectantly, but the man makes no move to help him up. As Parker prepares to do the job himself, a different hand comes down. Natasha's. He takes it and she pulls him to his feet, then carries his crutches to him. She exits the doctor's dining room and he swings awkwardly after her to the front door, which opens onto a set of steps and a sidewalk. It's dark out, and the street is relatively empty.

"What time is it?" Parker asks.

Natasha looks at her phone. "Nine PM."

Nine. It's been four hours since they got off work.

Natasha closes the doctor's door and stands with her hands in her pockets. "How's the foot?" she asks.

"Gone."

"You know what I mean."

"Yeah. It's . . . fuck. All my life, I had a foot. Now I don't. What the fuck am I supposed to do with that?"

"I don't know."

Parker sits on the steps. He doesn't feel ready to be moving yet.

"Thank you," he says.

Natasha sits beside him. "I wasn't about to let you die."

"How'd you find that doctor so quick?"

"He's a friend of a friend."

"He didn't say how much I owe him. Does he know how to get a hold of me?"

"Don't worry. I already paid."

"Wait." Parker shakes his head. "Natasha, no. You can't do that for me."

"I can. I did."

"How much *was* it?"

"I have more money than you realize. Inheritance."

"Even so—"

She takes his arm in her hand. She looks into his eyes. "Listen. It doesn't matter how much it was. It was worth it. You're alive."

For the first time, Parker sees Natasha, *really* sees her. Before, he'd look at her and see an annoying coworker who wouldn't shut up about her sandwich. Today, they'd moved past that, and he began to look her and see a friend. Now, he looks at her and finally, he sees a woman. A strong, intelligent, and beautiful woman. A woman who saved his life. From the look in her eyes, he knows she's feeling something similar.

He didn't think he'd ever fall for Natasha, of all people, but things have been pretty weird lately. This doesn't even crack the top fifty. And it feels right. For once—maybe it's the near-death experience helping him to reevaluate some things—it feels truly, totally *right*. Like maybe it's time to get off that treadmill chasing Charlotte and move on. So, he leans in toward her. She leans toward him.

"Wait," she says. She pulls back. "I just don't know if I can get over the sandwich thing."

"Are you serious?" Parker could just about smack her with his crutches. "What is *with* you and your stupid sandwiches?"

"You don't understand how amazing that mustard is! And it's so, *so* hard to come by. They only seem to have it in the store once every couple of months!"

Parker's heard it all, perhaps literally, thousands of times. "Whatever," he sighs. "I should have known better than to think that was going somewhere." Not like he hasn't been lifted up just to have his heart crushed before. "You'd think a guy would learn, eventually." He stands, picks up his crutches. "I'll admit, I have self-esteem issues. I don't always think so highly of myself. But at least I know I'm worth more than some stupid, goddamn *mustard*."

He swings away, ready to finally get home and be done with today.

Parker's apartment complex doesn't have an elevator, and if it did, there's no chance he would trust such a thing to take him safely between floors. Getting up the stairs is a total bitch. After his arms tire out, he goes down on his hands and knees and crawls the rest of the way. He's pretty sure he can feel the mold wriggling beneath his palms. It takes him three or more minutes to ascend when it took just twenty seconds before.

Mrs. Plymouth awaits Parker at the top of the stairs, but does not say hello. Her precious Milton has assimilated her into its biomass. Ensconced in heavy green fur, her glassy eyes are open but will never see again.

Oddly, she is smiling.

Parker wakes in the morning and stands to go to the restroom as he always does first thing. In drowsiness he puts his right "foot" down, forgetting it's a duck, and loses his balance. He topples to the floor.

"Hey there," says the man beneath his bed.

Parker shrieks.

"Hey, don't be scared. I'm just here to take you to my boss."

The man slides out from under the bed. Parker kicks out with his duck; the man blocks it. He stands, holding a pocket-sized spray bottle. Parker moves to knock the bottle away, isn't fast enough. A mist of clear liquid hits him in the face.

And he loses consciousness again.

CHAPTER SIX

A **DARK DUSTY ROOM**. A musty smell. Scattered holes in the wall admit a stippling of light, enough to show shelves stocked with various implements. Hedge clippers, a sickle, a rake. Gardening supplies.

Parker tries to move and finds he's unable. Cold metal clasps his wrists and his remaining ankle. He's been chained to the wall.

"Parker?"

Parker's blood goes cold. He'd hoped the owner of that voice had been buried under rubble, never to bother him again.

"Mia. You're the 'boss' that guy mentioned? How the hell do you have henchmen?"

"No. Look. I'm chained, too."

He turns to her, on his right. He strains his eyes against the dark and sees that she's telling the truth.

"What's going on here?" he asks.

"It's my—"

The door to the shed bursts open, and light floods inside. A tall man in a tweed shirt and glasses enters. He wears a brown leather satchel over on a strap over his shoulder. His appearance is unassuming, but something about the way the man carries himself tells Parker this is the "boss."

"Hello," the man says, in a pleasant tone harboring concealed malignance. "I see that you're nervous. That's understandable. When I was young, I used to get the jitters too when going to meet a girlfriend's parents for the first time."

Mia's . . . father? Parker looks at her, then shudders. The light reveals purple splotches on her face and neck. She may have acquired some of those bruises in the collapsing building, but Parker suspects this man has done the brunt of it.

"It's true," Mia says, sensing Parker's skepticism. "This here's my dear old daddy." She laughs bitterly. "Who doesn't love a family reunion?"

"You may call me Tony, if you wish," her father says.

"You shouldn't beat your daughter, Tony," Parker says. "It's shitty."

Tony's expression turns more severe. "Perhaps my daughter should not have run away, leaving me to think her dead for ten straight years. I only learned she was still alive from a news report about the havoc she wreaked on a building downtown. Surely, you can understand why I was upset. Why I was 'shitty,' as you put it. It brings me no joy to inflict pain on my own flesh and blood, but when lines are crossed so grievously, they must be redrawn with force."

"I can't possibly imagine why she would've run away from you," Parker says.

"Careful now," Tony says. "See how you are shackled, and I am not? See how I have two feet, and you do not? Deference may prove a wiser strategy for you. Or have you decided you're not yet crippled enough?"

Parker says nothing.

Tony acknowledges his silence with a nod. "The natural order resumes. Excellent."

"Why am I here?" Parker asks.

"You, my dear Parker, are here to assist me in a business operation."

Tony's a drug distributor. That's not all he does—he's got his hands in just about every criminal enterprise imaginable—but this particular job is about drugs. Tony has a client who owns an out-of-city motel that's basically just a front for a bunch of gangster bullshit. This motel owner's put in a bulk order for a drug known, unofficially, as Fentanyl 4, supposedly the craziest sequel yet to the drug that ravaged the country during Parker's childhood.

That's where Mia comes in. Apparently, if you hook her up to a freight container in her truck form and load it full of goods, the goods are hidden but don't disappear when she reverts back to human. They'll still be there when she turns back into a truck. It makes her a perfect asset for smuggling illicit material.

As for Parker's role, according to the new law, Mia's not allowed to leave the city without him. If she does, she'll be viewed as attempting to flee her obligation. Tony doesn't want anyone from the DFPE nosing in on his business, so Parker's got to go with her.

After explaining the details, Tony leaves them. A few long moments pass.

"I'm sorry, Parker," Mia says, breaking the silence. "For everything."

Parker suspected this apology would come, sooner or later. It's obvious, being the kind of person she was, she'd try to manipulate him back to her side by saying she's sorry. What a load of crap. Janice is still dead. He still has a duck for a foot. Sorry changes nothing.

"Fuck you and fuck your apology," he says. "I'm done with your games."

"I really am—"

"Stop talking. I was much happier pretending you're not here."

Silence returns to the room. Time treads on and the light through the wall goes dim, then out, and in the dark the silence grows thick and foul and at last Parker can bear it no longer.

"What you've done to me, I can't forgive," he says. The silence flees like a great weight lifted from the air. "But that doesn't make it right, him beating you, chaining you up and using you. You don't deserve that."

"You're okay with me talking now?" Mia asks.

"I thought I liked the quiet better. I was wrong."

"The beating's nothing new," Mia says. "Tony's always been this way. He first used me to smuggle drugs when I was four years old."

"Wow. I'm sorry."

"As an infant, I didn't have any control over my transformations. I'd turn into a truck and back again at random, which me a very difficult child to take care of. I killed five babysitters by accident before my dad—no, I refuse to call him that—before *Tony* bought a garage big enough to fit me." She pauses. "You don't mind if I tell you about all this?"

Parker shrugs, which is stupid because she can't see him. "I should learn as much as I can about the man we're dealing with."

"Okay, so like I was saying, Tony built a garage for me. He kept me there until I became old enough to control myself. Then he roped me into the family business."

"Where was your mother?"

"My 'mother' was just a plain old truck, not even sentient."

"I don't understand."

"Tony has a special power. He can impregnate inanimate objects. The way I've always heard him tell it, he found out at the age of thirteen when he had a wet dream and got his underwear pregnant. The underwear gave birth to a little baby girl, who could, herself, transform into underwear. You know what Tony did with that baby girl, his very first child?"

Based on what Parker's heard so far, his guess was "something horrible."

"He flushed her down the toilet," Mia says. "And laughed about it."

"Holy shit."

"He's always been rotten, from day one. It's no surprise he got into his current line of work. I'm not his only child. There are many of us. He just needs to rub his sperm on something, anything, and he has another half-human, half-whatever to do his bidding. He wants an army of people who can shoot bullets from their hands or mouths? All he's got to do is do the nasty with a bunch of guns. He wants a henchman who can stay at his side and turn into a glass of lemonade when he's thirsty so he doesn't ever have to walk all the way back into the house to pour himself some? Easy. The kids go from conception to birth in less than two weeks on average. He's even discovered that if he forces two of these 'object people' to procreate, the resulting offspring will be able to transform into *both* objects. He's got a whole bunch of inbred kids serving double functions, like a toothbrush and hairdryer in one, for instance."

Parker recalls the thought he had while talking to that woman at the school. About how the notion of "more people" as a solution to a problem reduces people to mere tools. Tony represents the purest encapsulation of that way of thinking, microcosmic of everything that's wrong about the country's response to the Decline.

"I think my 'mother' must've had a major mechanical defect," Mia says. "Something that in me translates to a broken mind. I never wanted to kill Janice or, or cripple you." Her voice tremors as she fights to get the words out. She sniffles. "But it's like—like there's this other person inside of me, and she's certifiably batshit. I've tried medication, but it doesn't work. Therapy hasn't been much use, either. I know . . . nothing I've just told you excuses what I've done, but I wanted you to know. That I would . . . I would give . . . *any*thing to take it back." Mia's composure shatters, and she breaks down into heavy sobs. Between convulsive heaves she chokes out the words, "I'm sorry. I'm sorry."

Her flood of tears washes Parker's anger away. This is

no manipulation. Never before has he witnessed such a visceral outpouring of heartbreak and pain. Here is not a monster but a woman broken, through cycles of trauma and tragedy like hammers to the glass windows of her soul; here is a woman who has never been told that she's worth something, that she's good enough, that she doesn't need to hate herself.

"I forgive you," he says.

"That means a lot. Thank you."

"You're welcome."

"So, how about you? Since we're on this track already. Any tragedy in *your* past that you've been doing your best to avoid?"

"I dunno . . . "

"Come on. *I* shared. It feels good to get it out."

Ah, screw it. It's been a long time since he's talked about this, and maybe he should.

"Fell in love in my late teens," he says. "Girl named Charlotte. Back then, before World War 3, before there was a new pandemic every year and everything with the climate and so on, we had a lot of optimism about the future. We wanted kids, and we wanted them young. Charlotte got pregnant at twenty, then . . . "

He takes a deep breath. Here came the difficult part.

"I thought it was weird that Charlotte refused to let me go with her to her ultrasound appointments, even refused to let me see the pictures. It was even weirder how quickly the pregnancy progressed. But I didn't know what was truly going on until she gave birth to the children in our bed—all twenty of them. You see, Charlotte had hidden from me the fact that she was actually half spider. A black lace weaver spider, specifically. She told me it had something to do with a mad scientist and a lab. Do you know what happens when black lace weaver spiders are born?"

"No."

"They eat the mother."

Mia gasps.

"I walked in on the sight of them tearing her to pieces. That was when, with her last breaths before she died, she told me the truth. She'd kept it a secret from me because she knew that if I knew, I'd say no to having children. The children were more important to her than her life."

"Is that why you . . ."

"Why I said I wasn't ready for a relationship. Yeah. Well, that and the fact you'd put a knife at my throat earlier in the day."

"I'm so sorry. What happened to the children?"

"They scuttled away on all their many legs and vanished. I found one of them dead in the street after searching, hit by a car. I never found the others."

"Oh!" Mia shouts. "The CB radio!"

Parker frowns at the non-sequitur. "Huh?"

"I got a CB radio installed inside me for use during emergencies. Tony doesn't know it's there."

Parker wonders what it was he said that reminded her she had a radio inside herself. Regardless, it seems they're done spilling their guts for now. She was right—it *did* feel good to get it out.

"Let me just . . . okay, got it." Something clatters to the floor. "I can't change the channel without the rest of the device, and it's too big to pull out of me like this, so we'll just have to hope someone's listening on the channel it's tuned to."

"Doesn't Tony have anyone keeping tabs on us to make sure we don't try anything like this? How do we know he's not already on his way to come cut my fingers off or something?"

"Oh, Tony would do *way* worse than cut off your fingers."

"That's not helping."

"Sorry. Anyway, I think he'd have come by now. He's arrogant, and he might think there's no point because he believes there's no chance we can escape, and any schemes we might come up with while talking with each other won't make a difference."

Parker hopes she's right.

"Do you want to talk, or should I?" she asks.

"You go ahead."

"Okay." A click. "Hello. I am being held against my will and am in need of help. This is an emergency. If anyone is listening on this channel, please respond. I repeat, I am being held against my will and am in need of help."

They wait for a response. Then the radio crackles and a man says, "This is Rusty Nail."

Parker gets a sinking feeling. He can guess what this asshole is up to, and hopes to God he's wrong.

"Rusty, hi, thank you so much for responding," Mia says. "I can't tell you what it means to hear another voice. So, listen, my friend and I are being held—"

"Candy Cane? Hey, anybody know a Candy Cane?" Rusty Nail asks.

Goddamnit. Parker hates being right sometimes.

"I'm sorry, I don't follow," Mia says.

"He thinks he's being funny," Parker says. "Here, let me see that."

Mia hands him the speaker, which is slick with her saliva. "Listen, 'Rusty Nail,'" he says.

"You have to hold down the button on the side," Mia says.

Parker finds the button and presses it. "We're not playing a game here, okay? This is serious."

"Where's my Candy Cane?" Rusty Nail asks. "I got the pink champagne!"

"For God's sake, fuckhead, we are *in danger*. Quit quoting that stupid fucking movie at us and help us out!"

"Caaaaaandy caaaane," Rusty Nail says.

"Shit!" Parker throws the CB.

"Hey, that hurt," Mia says. "It's part of my intestines."

"Sorry."

"What was that about? What movie?"

"It's an old horror film called *Joy Ride.* Some guys get a CB radio in their car and play a prank on a truck driver, who turns out to be—whatever, it doesn't matter. We're screwed."

The radio crackles again. "Hello?" A woman's voice. "Hello, are you still there?"

Mia picks it up. "Yes!" she practically shouts. "Yes, we're still here. Can you help us?"

"I'll try harder than that other guy. Geez, 'Rusty Nail?' That movie's over fifty freakin' years old. I'm Camila, by the way."

"Thank you. Thank you so much. My friend and I, we're being held at the east end of the city. About a mile past where Faxcole Avenue becomes Highway 719, there's a big, gaudy compound off to the right of the road. It's impossible to miss. You'll see a tall, lit-up sign that says 'Tony Town'—"

"Oh, I know that place. I always thought it was a family fun center or something."

"That's about as far from what it is as can be, but I see how you got that impression."

"What do you want me to do? Should I notify the police?"

"Scared of or working with Tony. I don't think we could count on them to show up in less than a few hours, anyway."

"I've got an idea," Parker says. "Look up the number for the Department of Fertility and Population Expansion. Tell them we're two partners who are unable to fulfill our sexual obligations because we're being held against our will. Tell them where. They'll lose their shit. Also, call my friend, her name's Natasha. Her number is . . . " He thinks about it, struggling to remember. "555-484-8100. I think. Tell her the situation. Maybe there's something she can do."

"Okay," Camila says. "I'll give it a go."

"Thank you so much," Mia says.

The call ends. Parker leans back against the wall and stretches out his feet. All they can do now is wait.

Sometime not much later, Tony comes to the shed. Though it's nighttime, light shines bright through the open door behind him. "We're accelerating our timeline," he says.

"Why?" Mia asks.

"Some suit from the Department of Fertility and Population Expansion showed up. Somehow, they figured out you two are here. Insisted I'm 'obstructing humanity's survival,' or some such hogwash. Naturally, I fed him to my gators, but his friends in the government may not be so happy about . . . " He frowns, turns to look behind him. "What is that noise?"

Parker hears it too. The faraway roar of an engine, drawing closer. The rotor-blade whir of a helicopter. A man's voice booms, "Anthony Monroe! You are under arrest! Come quietly, or we will take you by force!"

Tony unzips his satchel and pulls out a slim dry-erase marker. The marker transforms into a bullhorn. This must be one of those "double function" children Mia spoke of. Tony may have dozens of markers in that satchel, each able to become a larger object at his behest. The colors of the markers would help him to remember which is which. He probably uses the bullhorn for shouting at his kids.

He steps outside, shed door swinging shut behind him, and speaks through the bullhorn: "Have you forgotten, gentlemen? I've been granted full immunity on account of my ability to mass-produce people with transformation capabilities. I was told that I could do, and I quote, 'whatever the hell I want.' Was that guy I killed really so special?"

"Regardless of what aid you rendered in the past, your current detainment of certain persons constitutes an obstruction of expansion. We will not hesitate to make an example of you if we must."

Tony tosses aside the bullhorn and flips off the helicopter.

An explosion rocks the compound.

"Hey!" Tony whines. "You just blew up my water slide!"

"More of your fancy bullshit will be next if you don't cooperate!"

"Now," Mia whispers. Two snaps sound in quick succession, followed by metal hitting the floor.

"Did you just break your shackles?" Parker asks.

"Yep."

"Have you been able to this whole time?"

"Of course."

"I just assumed something was hindering you."

"Why would you assume that?"

"Because, if you could've become a truck all this time, why the hell *haven't* you?"

"Tony's not stupid. He knows what I can do and he has a hundred was to stop me if I do it. The shackles aren't here to literally restrain me, they're merely meant to symbolize the fact that I'm trapped. But now, we've got a distraction."

She brings a metal fist down on his chains, breaking them. Facing the door, she strides forward, enlarging as she does so. The structure of her body changes from that of a woman to a hulking mechanical beast. She blows through the wall of the shed as if it's made of paper. Outside, Tony stands bathed in floodlight, watching the hovering helicopter. Mia charges at his back.

A man leaps into Mia's path, a seemingly suicidal maneuver explained by his becoming a steel wall, stopping Mia dead with a crash.

"Owch!" Mia howls. It must hurt just as it would if Parker were to bash his own face against a wall. But Mia, undeterred, backs up to try a different tactic.

An ear-shattering *boom* shakes the world as the sky ignites in a sun-bright blossom of orange. A cataclysm of fire, metal and glass rains onto the concrete. A piece of burning shrapnel lands in front of Parker, and he shrieks, scrambling backward.

Next, the rattle of gunfire. Parker crawls to the open side of the shed for a closer look. Tony's slipped away, but his children have stayed to battle government agents as they arrive at the compound. Holes punch into bodies and they fall and lay bleeding, gasping, twitching, as combat rages over them.

More of Tony's children enter the fray. A woman becomes a pitchfork and gores a man on her tongs. A man turns into a steamroller and flattens friends and foes alike, too big for precise control. Another woman turns into a five-foot-by-two wooden desk and sits for a moment, doing nothing, until she catches a rocket and explodes.

The shed's missing wall leaves Parker exposed. He searches for another spot to hide. The compound's layout is insane. Everything, including the kitchen sink—literally, in an open-air kitchen off to the right of the shed—has been thrown together without rhyme or reason. Past the kitchen, a massive gold statue of Tony overlooks an Olympic-size swimming pool with the remnants of a slide smoldering in the water.

Statue. Huge, solidly-built—good for cover. Parker leaves the shed and crawls toward the pretentious effigy.

A man in a clown costume jumps into Parker's path. "You're not going *any*where, pal!" the man shouts, then turns into a plate of spaghetti.

The plate leaps onto Parker's face. Pasta sauce oozes into his mouth, nose, and eyes, blinding him. Limp angel hair strands wriggle on his skin like worms. He rips off several and stuffs them in his mouth, chews them, swallows. The spaghetti resumes the form of a man, but now, he's missing an arm. Instead of blood, more pasta sauce gushes from the ragged stump below his shoulder.

"You—you *ate* my arm!" the man shrieks. "You freak! You cannibal!"

"You were attacking me," Parker says.

"I'll *kill* you!"

As hard as he can, Parker drives his metal duck-foot into the man's testicles. The man goes down howling. Parker crawls the rest of the way to the statue.

Army tanks like big metal long-snouted turtles on treads have joined the battle, cannons unleashing a barrage of mayhem. A fighter jet sweeps overhead in a hail of gunfire, loops around and passes again. A cloud of smoke and debris rises and washes over the compound.

A horn sounds and truck-form Mia careers into sight. She zigs and zags, out of control, toward the statue. Her brakes squeal, and she slows, but not enough. Metal meets metal in a deafening crash. Mia shrinks down as Parker rushes to her side. She wobbles, nearly falling. He grabs her and helps her sit down.

"*Fuck,* that hurt," she says, holding the side of her face. She's bleeding from . . . just about everywhere. "I took a lot of damage out there. All systems shot—heh. Figuratively *and* literally. I can't stay here, though. Need to help. Gotta give Tony what's coming to him."

"I don't think that's a good idea," Parker says.

"We're going to lose. I can feel it."

"*You're* going to die if you push yourself anymore."

"I can keep going. I—"

"Tony Town residents!" a woman bellows, loud enough to be heard even through the calamity. Parker recognizes her voice straight away—it's Camila. She must be using the PA system in her truck. "Did someone here order from Bildo's Dildos?"

But Camila can't be in her truck. The voice is up *above* them. In the sky, silhouetted against the moon, a zeppelin floats over the compound.

"Because we've got a whole assortment of goodies for you!" another woman shouts. Natasha.

"Here're our reinforcements," Parker says. "Let's see what they've got before you rush out there and get yourself killed, okay?"

"Okay," Mia says. "I'll rest."

The zeppelin shits something out its bottom. Seconds later, hundreds upon hundreds of banana peels hit the ground. Curious, Parker picks one up, but it immediately slips free of his hand. He tries again, same result. Banana peels, engineered to be extra slippery; leave it to Bildo's Dildos to make a weapon inspired by cartoon logic.

Then—Parker's sensing a theme here—a deluge of banana cream pies that explode upon impact. After a minute or so of this dessert bombardment, a rubber chicken falls. It hits the ground, squawks, and lays there just long enough to make Parker think it's a dud. Then, with more squawking, it jumps to its feet and sprouts a proliferation of horror: sharp spines, tentacles, gooey eyes and lilting tongues. The nightmare creature runs into the fray. Parker looks away the moment the screams begin.

The fight rages on. More comical weaponry drops onto the battlefield—large anvils, killer chocolate bunnies, gargantuan cheese wheels that roll around on their own. Eventually, the zeppelin flies away, its stores depleted. The air is filled with dust and smoke and the anguished moans of the dying.

Boom.

The earth rumbles.

Boom.

"What the hell *is* that?" Parker asks.

Boom. Boom.

They're not explosions. More like the sound of something impossibly heavy hitting the ground over and over, at near-perfectly even intervals, almost like . . . footsteps.

Looming over the buildings, a colossal reptilian kaiju like something out of a Godzilla film gazes down with one orange, quivering eye. The living skyscraper's pustuled red lips open and it speaks, to Parker's amazement and dismay, in a voice that, although tremendously louder than before, is unmistakable. Somehow, the monster is none other than Tony himself.

"Where are you, Parker? Mia?"

"You didn't tell me he could turn into a giant mutant," Parker whispers to Mia.

"I didn't know."

"Come on out!" Tony calls. He lifts a green-scaled foot the size of a minivan. Even the claws are bigger than Parker. The foot glides forward and plants down in the carpet of bodies. *Boom.*

"I'll go," Mia says, standing up.

"What?" Parker grabs her. "No. Don't be an idiot. We need to *run* from that thing."

"I've *been* running from that monster for a long time now. One way or another, he and I end this now."

"Fucking hell, Mia. How are you even going to stop him?"

"Remember what I told you back in that building, before I fell through the floor? I have a self-destruct system."

Parker shakes his head. "No, come on. It's not worth your life. There's got to be some other way."

"We leave him now, he'll just start building his army again. He'll go on destroying countless lives until the day nature finally comes for him, and I'm not even sure he won't find a way around *that*. No. I end him, now."

Parker opens his mouth. Closes it. A thousand objections sit at the tip of his tongue, yet not one of them is worth a damn. He can't stop a woman who can turn into a semi-truck. And goddamnit, but she's right.

She gives him one last, long look, full of sadness, and says, "I know you totally lied out your ass about liking honey badgers because you couldn't think of anything else. But I thought it was cute. And that moment outside your apartment, when you gave me your mold mask instead of using it yourself? That was just about the sweetest thing anyone's ever done for me. That was the moment I fell in love with you. I guess some things just aren't meant to be, though. That other woman, the one I didn't kill, what's her name? Natasha? You should be with her. You like her, don't you?"

"She only cares about her stupid mustard," Parker says.

"She'll come around."

Mia walks around to the front of the statue.

"Ah, daughter," Tony says. "There you are. This insubordination of yours has gone quite far enough. I shall have to keep you on a far, *far* shorter leash from now on."

"If you want a dog, Tony, just fuck one," Mia says. "You can't put a *truck* on a *leash*."

She goes to truck form. Parker thinks he hears her say one last thing, but it's hard to make out over the growl of her engine. She accelerates forward.

"What are you doing?" Tony asks.

She picks up speed, closes the distance. Tony opens his mouth to say something more.

He never gets the chance. Parker throws himself down and covers his ears as Mia hits Tony's leg and explodes like a miniature supernova. The sound is beyond deafening. Even at this distance, the shockwave hits Parker like a strong wind, blowing dust into his face.

Seconds later, Parker is buried in a thick and tangy liquid that fills his lungs and steals away his consciousness.

He awakes on a familiar dining room table, Natasha's doctor friend standing over him.

"You're lucky to be alive," the doctor says.

"What happened?" Parker asks.

"You essentially drowned in a large quantity of mustard."

"Mustard?"

"Yes. Natasha saw it happen. She says your truck girlfriend made the big guy explode. Apparently, his insides were made of mustard, which then rained down on you."

"I almost drowned in a guy's guts?"

"Almost. But not quite. You're alive, but there's, uh, one little thing. You ingested *so much* mustard, that *your* insides are now mustard. No organs, no blood—you still have bones, but the rest is basically *all* condiment."

"How the hell am I not dead?"

"Honestly? Don't know. Natasha's waiting for you outside."

As the doctor said, Parker finds Natasha waiting on the steps. The moment he swings out the door on his crutches, she stands, takes him in her arms, and kisses him.

"I'm sorry," she says, after she pulls away. "Me and my mustard fetish . . . the thing is, it started when I was a girl . . . "

"Is this a sob story?" Parker asks.

"Very much so."

"Tell it to me later. I've had enough tragedy today."

"The point is, I fucked up. I like you, Parker. It's rare for me to say this, but . . . you *are* worth more to me than mustard. And I forgive you for eating my sandwich."

"I like you, too," Parker says. "Also, my insides are mustard now. So, you might just be getting the best of both worlds."

"That's wild," she says. She sniffs, and her eyes go wide. "It's my special mustard!"

"You can smell my insides?"

"Yep. How are you not dead, by the way?"

"Doctor said he had no clue. How did *you* get all that stuff from Bildo's Dildos?"

"I promised to have sex with the guy who was working the store. Mind you, I'm not actually gonna *do* it."

"Heh, what an idiot. Bet you he's getting fired."

"Say, speaking of sex . . . " Natasha's eyes sparkle. "Is your cum made of mustard, too?"

"No clue."

"Do you . . . wanna find out?"

"I've had a rough few days. Give me a little time?"

"Okay. No problem." She kisses him again. "I can wait."

"Hey! *Hey!*" A man rushes over to them. "What the *fuck* do you think you're doing?"

"Oh, it's my assigned partner," Natasha says. "You know what? After kicking that guy Tony's ass, I'm in a 'fuck it' mood." She pulls a gun out of her purse and shoots the man in the head.

"Wow," Parker says.

"He deserved it."

"The DFPE won't like that very much."

She shrugs. "We'll cross that bridge when we come to it. Wanna get coffee?"

"Sure. As long as it doesn't have gasoline."

ABOUT THE AUTHOR

Riley Odell is an autistic neurodiversity advocate and writer of horror, comedy, bizarro, and stories about autism. His second horror collection, *Vile Visions Volume 2*, was nominated for a 2025 Wonderland Award, celebrating superior achievement in bizarro fiction. He edited and published *Divergent Realms: Science Fiction and Fantasy Stories About Neurodivergence*, an anthology of fourteen stories about neurodivergent characters, written by neurodivergent writers. He is also the madman responsible for *Bizarro Circus of Madness*, an anthology of twenty-one bizarro fiction stories. He lives in Fort Collins, Colorado, with his wife Jamie and their two pet children, a dog named Sadie and a rabbit named Newton.

* 9 7 8 1 9 6 7 5 1 7 1 7 6 *

MY WEIRD
NIGHTMARE BABY

RILEY ODELL

Madness Hearts Press

My Weird Nightmare Baby
Copyright © 2026 Riley Odell

All Rights Reserved

Cover by Betty Rocksteady

CHAPTER ONE

ANOTHER SLAB OF meat goes through the machine and becomes dentures. I examine the glossy white resin teeth and find no imperfections. They are ready.

Another slab. The machine's pipe belches a jaundice-yellow, acrid cloud of steam. It's a sauna in here. My sweat's glued my clothes to my skin. Above, an industrial-sized fan sucks up the muggy, stinking air and somehow sends back air that's muggier and stinkier.

I pick up the next set of dentures.

Chomp.

"Ow!" I throw them on the ground. *Shit. Not good.* I bend to pick them up, but they scamper away, clacking, and vanish into a mouse hole.

Shit. That's coming out of my paycheck.

Oh well. I return to the conveyor and continue my work. Slab after slab of meat passes by. Meat, meat, meat . . . and then something that isn't. At least, isn't dead. It's my coworker, Jimbob.

"Jimbob, get off," I say.

I almost let him through without noticing. Jimbob's got that look some people have where you can hardly tell them apart from a cut of prime rib. I think it's the skin discoloration that does it. From the necrosis.

"I want to be dentures," Jimbob says.

I turn off the conveyor. "We need you, Jim. We're short-staffed."

"I want to be dentures."

"We don't know what will happen if you go through that machine. We don't even know how it works."

The machine is a big metal box that makes noise. It turns meat into dentures, and that's all anybody knows.

"I want to be dentures."

"It's good to have dreams, Jim. Now come down."

Jimbob climbs off the belt and grumbles away to his station. I start the machine up again.

Meat, dentures, repeat. The process makes me hungry. I think I'll have steak tonight.

A little boy is on the conveyor, riding it like a roller coaster. "Whee!" he exclaims.

I pull him off. "It's not a ride, kid."

He gives me pouty eyes. "I'm telling Mom you were mean."

"You do that."

I turn the machine off and head for the bathroom. The path meanders through a maze of conveyors and other machines, most of which do nothing. The overhead lights coat the metal surfaces in a nauseating fluorescent sheen.

Dick and Mick are at the big metal bar you've got to pull back and forth, requiring two people. Nobody has any inkling of what that one does, but it's supposedly important. Klaus is working on the machine that prepares the meat. Three days ago, he lost his right arm to that machine. Now he's got his other arm wedged deep in its guts, trying to fix some problem. Hopefully, the "OFF" button works this time.

I reach the bathroom and knock on the door. "Occupied," the man inside says.

"Open up, please, sir."

The door opens a smidge and a stack of chins peeks out. If you peer closely at the flab, you can make out a face.

"You're not to disturb me while I'm on the toilet," he says. His manifold folds jiggle with the movement of his jaw.

"You're always on the toilet. You converted the bathroom into your office."

MY WEIRD NIGHTMARE BABY

"And you're not getting the message. What is it? Why are you bothering me?"

"People are getting on the conveyor again."

"Jimbob?"

"And a little boy."

"I'll look into it."

"What about the kid?"

"Just deal with it."

When I return, the kid's mom is there. She's standing in a cluster of infants, six of them, all bawling hysterically. One look at the scene and I shudder, taking a step back.

"How dare you treat my kid that way," she says.

"Control him," I snap at her. "He nearly became dentures."

"Maybe that's what he wants," she says. "Did you consider that?"

A baby crawls towards me. I retreat farther, my back pressing against the conveyor.

"What's your problem?" the mother demands.

The baby continues to encroach.

"Get it away, please. Please," I say.

I'm rooted to the spot. The mother says something I can't make out. The baby barnacles onto my leg, the sensation like dipping the limb in mucus. The room spins, and in my mind, images flash of an event I've tried my whole life to forget. My father, standing on a bridge, waving, smiling, and behind him . . .

Briefly, there is darkness as my brain, overwhelmed, shuts itself off. When it comes on again, I'm on the floor, thrashing, screaming, "Get it off!" I re-seize control and stop. The mother stares, mouth agape.

"You're a freak," she says. "You kicked my baby."

"They all look fine to me."

"You're lucky," she says. "I could be pressing charges, but I won't. Just stay away from me and my family."

She loads her infants into a multi-seat wagon stroller and stomps away. The boy who started all this sticks his tongue out at me and then follows her.

The boss's voice booms over the loudspeaker: "Neil. My office."

Crud.

He's got a cooked-lobster complexion when he opens the bathroom door.

"What the fuck," he says.

"I'm sorry," I say. "Her baby. It came right at me."

He squints. "Her baby?"

"Yes. I have infantophobia—er, fear of babies, that is. See, my father . . . "

"That's not a real thing."

"Um. Yes, it is."

"It's not. Babies are small and fragile and cute. What you're saying is absurd."

"Sir . . . "

He sits on the toilet and farts. "I ought to fire you. She says you kicked her baby clear across the room."

"I don't remember exactly *what* happened, but surely that's an exaggeration."

"But you're a good employee, so I'll let you off with a warning."

"Thank you."

As I leave the bathroom, Klaus screams. Dick and Mick rush to see what's happened and I join them. Klaus is on the floor holding his left arm, or what's left of it. Blood is everywhere.

Just another day at work.

The streets are lively, but the crowds thin out as beleaguered workers plod back to their homes. The synthetic sun in the painted blue sky is dimming; soon it will turn off for the night.

I turn right at the New Mississippi waterfront. The river's a spinach-soufflé shade of green, sizzling and steaming with heat. Bubbles rise and pop like snapping teeth. It reeks like rotting farts.

4

MY WEIRD NIGHTMARE BABY

Shelves as wide as the streets stretch skyward, stocked with goods. I pass row after row of giant Crisco tubs. An elevator door opens, a man steps in, and the elevator shoots toward the upper shelves.

More shelves, their supports repurposed as canvases. Graffiti everywhere. Fuck the world, fuck the police. Always fuck something.

Trash and homeless people gather together due to lack of space: the trash in haphazard mounds, flooding into the streets; the homeless in tents, or lined up curbside, begging for change. Some of them have signs. "Hungry, please help." "Parents kicked me out, please help." "My life sucks."

A car blazes by. Cops in pursuit, *weeoo, weeoo,* lights atop flashing like disco's comeback. Their quarry nicks a shelf, spins out in a squeal. The driver steps out and stumbles, flopping into the road. He attempts to stand, and the police light him up. His body jerks as bullets strike him, dancing a bloody rendition of the worm.

I come to a bridge. Ordinarily, I would give this particular bridge a wide berth, but not today. Today, I feel drawn to the structure. The baby incident at work's got something to do with it, I suppose. I walk to the middle of the bridge and gaze out across the disgusting water.

This is where it happened. Mom, Dad and I went to the carnival, and on the way back Dad wanted to have his picture taken on the bridge. This was something of a famous landmark back then, when the water was cleaner.

The news blamed it on masturbathing—men jerking off in the shower. Thousands of gallons of jizz drained into the river, where thousands of people swam naked, unaware. The jizzwater mixed with chemicals from a spill at a nearby plant; swimmers became impregnated, with greatly expedited incubation. Instead of nine months, these babies went from zero to born in under five minutes. Hundreds of newborns cannonballed simultaneously from hundreds of vaginas—the chemicals were also highly lubricative.

The result was a tsunami of babies. I remember standing where I stand now, watching my dad smile and wave, and then seeing the wave behind him. I shouted at him to move, but it was too late. The babies cascaded onto the bridge, burying him.

I don't know why I came onto the bridge today. I should've just kept going.

Resuming my walk, I pass an overflowing orphanage. Children are spilling out the doors and windows onto the sidewalk. Passersby step around them as if they're not there.

A mother walks up to me with a stroller. A glabrous glob of flesh sits inside, wailing.

What is it with today? "Take him away, please," I say.

"Will you watch him for a moment?" she asks.

"He's your kid."

The baby's pudgy, flailing little hand brushes my knee. Black spots dance at the edge of my vision as panic threatens to usurp me again.

She sours. "It's just for a *moment.*"

"I don't care."

A second woman bumps into me. She has a toddler in tow. "Excuse me, sir?" she says.

"No!" I shout.

"But—"

A third swoops in from the left. Her baby is smooth and glossy white—a tooth. "Hello, I was wondering if you wouldn't mind—"

Everything spinning. Can't breathe. Going dark again. "I can't do this. Please, all of you, go away."

"Won't you please? He's teething. He's in a lot of pain," says the tooth mother.

A fourth woman joins, and I'm surrounded. This one proffers an oversized teratoma. It resembles lumpy, uncooked meat with teeth and eyes, and it's bawling like the world's about to end.

I back away. "Th—that's a tumor! What the hell?"

MY WEIRD NIGHTMARE BABY

"Why are you such an asshole?" screams the original assailant. She slaps me in the face. "We just need you to take care of our kids!"

"Fuck off!" I ram the nearest mother out of the way and sprint until I can't anymore. I stop, lungs burning. Shelves stocked with toilet paper, paper towels, and related items tower into the sky. I should be safe for the moment.

A hand grabs my ankle. "Neil!"

"Gah!" I shriek.

Mom's face pokes through an open manhole, grinning at me. "Where are my grandchildren, Neil?"

"Damnit, Mom! You have to stop ambushing me like this!"

"About those grandchildren . . ."

"You're not getting any!"

"Selfish prick! Stiffing your own mother!"

"Can you *please* just go away?"

"You've got to look around, Neil. Can't you see the world is a wonderful place? Depriving your future offspring of such joy would be . . . well, it would just be *wrong!*"

An anguished cry draws my attention away from her. A malnourished child of four or five, gender indiscernible, drags its emaciated body along the pavement. Buzzards circle the upper shelves, waiting for the child to croak.

"Help," the child groans.

"Oh, how horrible," an onlooker remarks.

The obese woman next to him stuffs a greasy hamburger in her mouth. "Such a shame there's nothing we can do."

The child produces a syringe and injects the green liquid contents into its arm.

"Oh dear, it's even addicted to drugs," the man says.

"Such a shame," the woman says.

From my right comes a hellish, inhuman squeal. Next to the toilet paper, a baboon tears into an antelope. Blood and guts go every which way.

"Isn't nature beautiful?" the woman says.

"It most certainly is," says the man.

He draws a gun from his pocket and shoots the woman in the head.

"Sorry, I just felt like doing that," the man says, and walks away.

"That's enough looking around for me," I say.

"So you're going to have children, then?" Mom asks.

"Bye, Mom."

I push her down with my foot. She loses her grip and screams as she plummets to the ground below. She'll be fine—she's resilient like that.

My apartment building's two blocks away. Inside, the grimy, stinking hallway is peeling, chipping, cracking, creaking. Trash of all kinds everywhere, from food to bottles to needles. Some needles lay alone, while others stick out from the tourniquet-tied arms of people who don't live here, but have nowhere else to go. They're here for refuge, but most deem them mere refuse.

My landlord is waiting for me outside my apartment.

"Your rent, Neil," he says. "You're overdue. As usual."

"I'm sorry. My boss reduced everyone's pay again."

"Not my problem. Get it to me by the end of the week."

He leaves. I enter the apartment and wade through the smegma of bottles and food containers to my recliner. It groans as I sit down. I turn on the TV, open a bag of chips, and begin to watch porn.

CHAPTER TWO

SOME NIGHTS when I can afford it, I go to Mackey's for a drink.

Mackey's is a homey little hole-in-the-wall sort of place, the sort you wouldn't know was there if you didn't know where to look. I enter and am greeted by jukebox jazz and the familiar scent-cocktail of beer, bad nachos, and stale vomit. Patrons sit and chat at dimly lit tables or stand playing pool. Some sit alone, mirrors of myself, wilted in face and body as though their souls have left them.

I take a seat at the bar. Mackey—a burly, mustachioed, one-eyed hulk of a man—finishes wiping up a previous customer's mess and turns to me.

"What will you be having tonight, Neil?"

"Shot of whiskey. And some of that poontang stuff."

"*Poutine,*" Mackey corrects.

"Yeah, that."

My friend Levi takes a seat on my left. He grins at me. "Poontang, huh?"

"I pronounced it wrong. Big deal."

"That's not just a mispronunciation. Thinking about sex, are you?"

"He's always thinking about sex." This new speaker is my other friend, Nick, who takes the stool on my right. "Poor Neil, no woman ever wants to sleep with him."

The jukebox skips, then screeches, jarring and loud. I grit my teeth. "This is not a discussion I want to have right now."

"*Oh,*" Levi says. "Bad day."

"Babies," I say.

"*Oh,*" Levi says.

"Here's your piss." Mackey hands me a glass of beer. "Here's your shit." He hands me a bowl of gravy-soaked french fries and cheese. "Ten dollars."

I give him my card and pick up the drink. It smells like detergent and doesn't taste much better. I down it in one gulp.

"You oughtta see a therapist about that issue of yours," Nick says.

"Been to plenty. Didn't work," I say.

"Alcohol works," Levi says.

"Why do you think I'm here?" Mackey's already brought another shot without me needing to ask. I take a swig. A warm, dull fuzziness sets in.

Drinks and small-talk topics come and go with equal swiftness. Soon I'm fuzzy as a bear and we've made our way, somehow, to the subject of giraffe copulation. Then Nick changes it again: "Neil, let's get you a babe."

Levi nods. "Yeah, man. Maybe it'll get you out of this slump of yours."

Nick points, not so subtly, to a group of women behind us. "Get in there," he says. "Win them over with your charms."

"I can't. Every woman wants babies. I can't deal with that."

"That's an excuse. You're just afraid of rejection," Levi says.

"Yeah. You don't know whether there aren't any women who don't want babies," Nick says.

"As if. That'd be like, one in a million."

"And maybe that one in a million is sitting *right there,*" Levi says.

"Maybe you're right."

He's right about rejection, too. When I do try, I always get rejected. Who would want to drive if they crashed every time they got in a car?

MY WEIRD NIGHTMARE BABY

I weigh whether I'm fuzzy enough to do this. I'm currently bear fuzzy; no less than mammoth fuzzy will do. I drink until I'm woolly, then consider it again.

"Okay," I say. "I'm ready."

Levi pats me on the back. "Go get 'em."

I walk over to the women. "Hi," I say.

"Fuck off," says a gorgeous brunette.

"Oh. Okay."

I fuck off back to my seat.

"*Dude*," Nick says. "Come on. You can do better than that."

"I said hi and she said fuck off."

"So you give up?" Levi says. "You want some jam to go with that milquetoast personality?"

"You didn't say it right," Nick says. "You gotta do it with pizzazz."

"Pizzazz?"

"Yeah. Like this."

He draws a pair of sunglasses from his pocket and puts them on. Then he lowers them, just enough for his eyes to show, and winks. "Hi," he says. The word drips with oily smarm so thick I can practically feel it on my skin. He nods to me. "Like that."

"I dunno," I say. "I'm gonna need to be a bit fuzzier for that."

So I fuzz myself up some more, until the room spins.

"Fix your floor," I say to Mackey. "It's wobbling again."

"Gonna have to cut you off soon," he says.

I gesture for Nick to give me the sunglasses. He hands them over with a wink. "Knock 'em dead," he says. I put them on and stumble to the women's table.

"H-hey," I say.

"Didn't you get the message?" the brunette's blonde friend asks.

"Oh geez," the brunette says. She looks down. Liquid leaks down her chair, pooling on the floor. I'm too drunk to have noticed it sooner, but she's clearly pregnant.

"What's wrong?" the blonde asks.

"My water just broke."

"Shit!" I exclaim. "Shouldn't you—"

The brunette jerks her head back and screams. "Gah! It hurts!"

"You're doing great, just push!" the redhead beside her says.

"Shouldn't you go to the hospital, or something?" I ask.

The blonde shoots me a glare. "You're still here? This is private, you know."

"But we're in a bar."

The brunette screams again. The wet tip of a head soaked in blood and amniotic fluid pokes from her crotch. What follows is more agonized howling as the brunette clutches the bottom of her chair, pushing with all her might. And then the tiny infant is free. The new mother takes her bawling bundle of misery in her arms and smiles as patrons clap and cheer from around the bar.

I wobble back to my seat. "It's too weird over there."

"Well, you gave it a shot," Nick says. He gives me a pat on the back.

"Have you tried online dating?" Levi asks.

Click.

Loretta9210. Damn, she's hot. She's got six kids, apparently.

Click.

Ven99. Eighty kids? What the hell?

Click.

TacoGirl. Her profile picture's a taco. That gives me nothing to work with.

LickMyButt84. Oh look, more kids.

Lovebird.com? They oughtta rename it womenwithkids.com.

A message pops up on the screen: "You must become

a subscriber to see more profiles." The cost is fifty dollars a month.

I move my cursor to the X in the corner.

Don't you want a date? I ask myself. *Don't you want to not be lonely anymore*?

What's fifty dollars? My happiness is worth at least that much. I pay it and continue.

The next profile catches my interest. Her username's LactosePink and she's got the nicest breasts I've ever seen. Plus, no kids.

A notification pops up to inform me that I've received a message. It's from LactosePink: "Hey. Saw you looked at my profile. Like what you see?"

Wow, that was fast. I click to reply and a different message pops up: You must pay to send messages to other users.

Apparently, sending messages will cost *another* fifty.

You need this, I tell myself. I pay it.

She writes: "I'm not appreciating the cold shoulder here. When I message you, I expect a reply."

What? It hasn't been a minute.

"Sorry, got blocked by a paywall. Yes, your profile interests me," I write.

"Oh. Sorry about that. I just get nervous. I think that when guys don't reply it's because they hate me and they want me to kill myself."

"Uh, well, I don't want that."

"Where do you want our first date to be?"

"I think you're getting ahead of yourself. Let's talk a bit first."

"What position do you like? Personally, I like to be fucked in the ass."

"Hold on. Slow down, okay?"

"What do you think we should name our kids? I'm thinking Harry if it's a boy. Or Jeffrey or Phil or Burt or Semen. Maybe Austin. Girl is Ashley, obviously."

"I don't think—"

There's a knock at the door. I leave the computer and open it. It's LactosePink—I recognize her from her photo.

"Are you ready?" she asks.

"Listen," I say. "This isn't going to work."

She frowns. "What?"

"You're insane."

Suddenly there's a knife in her hand. "I am *not*," she snarls.

She advances. Shit. My apartment's only got one exit, and she's standing in it. I scramble for something to defend myself with. Fleshlight? No. Porn mags? No. Masturbation sock?

Oh, right—my sledgehammer. I grab it off the wall and face LactosePink, swinging it to show I'm not fucking around. She backs up just far enough for me to run past. I ditch the hammer and sprint down the hallway, nearly running into my landlord.

"The rent, Neil!" he shouts after me.

"Sorry, psycho chasing me!" I shout back. "I'll talk later!"

I run into the street. LactosePink is close behind, growling like a rabid dog.

Mom appears from behind a trash bin and steps into the road, forcing me to run around her. She's got a cast on her leg from her fall the other day.

"What's going on, Neil?" she calls after me. "Running *away* from a woman isn't going to get me the grandchildren I'm owed! That's the exact *opposite* of what you should be doing!"

"Go away, Mom! Why does everyone think *this* is a good time to confront me?"

Brakes squeal. Mom screams. She's been mangled by a car, but LactosePink is still in pursuit. Then she screams, too. She's fallen into one of the gator pits the city keeps promising to eliminate.

I step around the pit and head back to my apartment.

"You haven't given us enough money," a lovebird.com

message informs me. "Give us more money if you want to keep using the site. Thank you."

The amount is a hundred dollars now. I pay it and continue to browse.

I find an ad for a speed dating event in the local paper. When I arrive at the venue, I find a group of plastic chairs arranged in a circle and fifteen people standing around, chatting.

A woman in a party hat walks to the front of the room. "Good evening, everyone," she says. "My name's Erica, and I'm in charge of this event. If you'll take your seats, I'll explain to you how it works."

We each find a seat in the circle.

"I'm going to put a song on the speaker, and while it's playing, I want you all to circle the outside of the ring. When it stops, sit in the nearest available chair—if there *is* one. Because, see, here's the fun part. As soon as I start the music, I'm going to remove a chair from the circle. That means *one* of you won't be able to sit back down. And if that happens, you're *outta here!*" She's super chipper as she explains this, grinning and making exuberant hand gestures. "But *if* you secure a seat, you get to talk to whoever's next to you for five minutes, until we start the next round!"

"Excuse me," I say.

"Yes?" Erica asks.

"That's just musical chairs, isn't it?"

"Yes, it is essentially musical chairs."

"And if you don't find a seat . . ."

"You have to leave."

"But I paid to be here! And the ad didn't say that it would be like this."

She frowns. "In order to create an authentic experience, we've designed the event to resemble dating in

the real world as closely as possible," she says. "I'm pretty sure it says *that* on the ad."

"Yes, but . . . I just didn't think . . . "

"Well, I'm sorry, but we can't offer you a refund."

"Fine."

She looks around the circle, grinning again. "Any other questions?"

No one has any, so she starts the music. We circle the chairs, ready to make our moves as soon as it goes quiet. Luckily, when it does, I'm able to snag a seat beside a beautiful blonde. The unlucky loser is a man on crutches, who looks ready to cry as he exits the room.

The blonde begins to talk with a hunk of a man on her other side. On my other side is an obese man in his fifties. I wait for a lull in the blonde's conversation and jump in with a, "Hello."

She turns to me. "Sorry," she says. "I'm talking."

The music starts again. This time, I hope to catch a seat alone next to one of the several attractive women in the group. When the music stops, I move to sit beside a brunette, but the hunk from before rams me out of the way and takes the seat for himself. I find myself instead between *two* obese, fifty-something men.

But the third time's the charm, they say. And indeed, fortune seems to smile on me—when the music stops, I'm close to a seat between the blonde and the brunette, and each has a woman on her other side. They'll have to talk to me, so long as they're not gay.

As I move to sit down, a man on roller skates barrels past and takes the seat. I curse—there are no seats left.

"Ouch," Erica says. "Better luck next time."

The next day after work, I visit the meat wall. The ninety-foot-tall structure sweats myoglobin in rivulets down its pink, spongy surface. I find my usual butcher, whose name

is Clive. He stands beside a sow stuck vertically in the wall, hooves forward, teats drooping like used condoms. He hefts a sledgehammer and smacks her in the skull with it; she squeals and dies.

"Whacha here for?" he asks me.

"Beef. Two pounds."

He takes a knife and cuts a couple slabs free from the wall, then packages them and hands them to me.

"Thank you," I say. I go to the nearest checkout lanes, at the intersection of Kensington and Farch. Casha the cashier picks up the meat and scans it with her forehead. She's a cyborg: up top a looker with brown hair, blue eyes, and plump breasts, while below, she's a metal box on wheels.

"Twenty dollars," she says.

I hand her the cash.

"Wanna fuck?" she asks.

Wait. "What?"

"I asked if you wanna fuck."

There's no way she really asked me that. No one has ever, *ever* asked me that. I must be hallucinating.

"What?"

She repeats it, annoyed this time. It really is what I thought I heard. She taps her metal exterior impatiently.

My throat is dry. I want to say yes. Instead: "I . . . " I swallow. "I . . . " I've forgotten the English language; I can only stare, dumbfounded. Is that my heart in my chest, or have I swallowed a marching band? "It's just . . . "

I can't tell her I've never done it before. She'd change her mind right away.

And what if I get her pregnant? *That's impossible. Her lower half isn't even human.*

"Fine," she says. "If you're not interested, just—"

"I'll do it!" I shout.

She rolls her eyes. "Men. Always so eager." She opens a panel on her front, revealing lumpy pinkish genitals. I join her behind the counter and she turns off the light to

indicate her lane is closed. She pulls a red curtain shut to grant us privacy.

"Okay," she says.

I unzip my pants. It takes a moment of finagling to align and insert myself, encountering more resistance than I expected. I go clumsily to work in her vagina, thrusting in and out until I ejaculate.

"That's it?" she says.

I pull out and zip up. "Did you like it?" I ask sheepishly.

"No," she says. "It was pathetic. What was that, twenty seconds?"

My shoulders deflate. "Oh."

"Go on. I need to work," she says.

"Would you . . . " I shuffle my feet. "Would you maybe like to get something to eat sometime?"

She laughs. Actually laughs, the sound like a knife to my gut. "With you? No. Now please." She flips the light on to indicate that lane 10,405,602 has reopened. "Leave."

CHAPTER THREE

I DREAM ABOUT Casha. We sit in the park together, enjoying ice cream, watching geese swim in the pond. I take a lick of my cookies and cream ice cream and hand it to her for her to try. She smiles and takes it. I rub her metal box lovingly.

"I love you," I say.

"I love you too," she says.

Thunder booms above. *That's strange*, I think. *It's such a nice day.* I look up. Black clouds churn, spiraling, a maelstrom in the sky. I look at Casha. Her face is blurred, distorted. "I hate you," she says.

She's holding a case of Stinky's Diapers.

I don't have time to think about why. There's an earsplitting wail, louder than thunder. The clouds part and a massive face peeks through. A baby's face.

I wake screaming in bed, drenched in sweat. I get up and go to the bathroom. My eyes are red and puffy in the mirror.

"Damnit!" I roar. I punch the glass, shattering it. My knuckles bleed.

I return to bed and toss and turn until I fall asleep, and dream about a man and woman copulating. There's thrusting, grunting, moaning. A rooster crows somewhere.

The man finishes. He pulls out.

"I'm scared," the woman says. "What if I get pregnant?"

The door to the room opens, and a man in a top hat

enters on a horse. He dismounts, draws a sword, and slaughters the animal. It topples with a scream, gouting blood. The man reaches into his pocket and withdraws a pack of Fojun condoms. "If you're worried about pregnancy, don't have unprotected sex. Wear Fojuns."

The woman looks at her sexual partner. "Did *you* wear a condom?" she asks.

"No," he says.

"Well then, that doesn't really help us," she says.

"I'm afraid *you're* screwed," the man in the top hat says. "Looks like you'll be dealing with one of *these* in your future." He removes the top hat and reaches inside, pulling forth a bawling infant. "Too bad! But for the rest of you: getting frisky is less risky with Fojuns!"

I wake up, and this time I'm infuriated. I didn't catch it with the diapers, but looking at the two dreams back-to-back, it's obvious: Those bastards are sending advertisements into my dreams again. I find my phone and dial a number.

"Sorry, don't feel like talking," a woman answers.

"What do you mean, you don't—"

She hangs up. I dial again.

"You again?" she says.

"My name is Neil Pierson and I'm on the 'no dream advertisements' list, do you understand? Tell them not to send advertisements into my dreams or I'll—"

She hangs up.

"*Shit!*" I guess I'll just have to go there myself.

The secretary is part human, part phone. Her right ear is a receiver, with a curly cord running down to a box at her waist. She's painting her nails as I walk into the lobby.

"I need to see your boss," I tell her.

"Oh," she says. "It's *you.*"

"Boss."

MY WEIRD NIGHTMARE BABY

"He's in there, but he's busy right now."

I storm to the indicated door and throw it open. The man inside has his penis in a jar of ketchup.

"You're just in time," he says. "I'm stuck. Could you help?"

"Why am I being shown advertisements in my sleep?" I demand. "I'm on the list! The list that says you can't do that!"

"That list no longer exists," he says.

"But I'm still paying money every month to be on it!"

"In that case, thank you for your contribution."

I hate this corporate runaround shit.

"Fine," I say. "Can you at least not send me dreams that have babies in them?"

He frowns. "You find babies objectionable?"

"I'm scared of infants. It's called infantophobia."

He laughs. "But babies are cute."

"Not to me. Babies killed my dad."

"You'll change your mind when you're older."

"I'm forty-five."

He narrows his eyes. "You're not joking, are you? You really hate babies."

"I don't *hate* them."

He rises from his chair and leans across the desk so his face is a foot from mine. This close, I can see the anger in his eyes. "I will *not* allow baby haters in my office. Get out."

"I—"

"Furthermore, our highly advanced algorithm determines what content to show you based on your *own* previous purchases."

"I haven't made any purchases like that."

He slams his palm on the desk. *"Out!"*

"Whatever."

I leave and make my way back home. 'Highly advanced algorithm' my ass. If it's so highly advanced, it ought to know I'm the last person in the world who wants to dream about babies. What's this purchase of mine that's got it so tripped up, anyway?

I bring up my email on my phone. Assuming such a purchase actually took place, I'd have been sent a receipt. I scroll through my unreads, not seeing anything—

"FREE BREAST ENHANCEMENT!" an email screams. I nearly throw the phone in shock.

"Dude, no one wants to hear about that," a passerby says.

"Fuck off," I snap. Stupid audio emails.

I mark the email as spam and keep going. Bills . . . newsletters . . . nothing. I type "baby" in the search bar. It brings up a receipt.

Meat—10 dollars

Baby—10 dollars

I click back. There are two emails above the receipt. The first's subject line says: "Your order is gestating."

And, "Your order is ready for pickup." I examine the details in the body of the email. One line catches my attention: "Please come to Lane 10,405,602 with your order number . . . "

Lane 10,405,602. Casha.

"Oh, look who finally decided to show," Casha says.

She places a crying infant on the counter. I yelp and yank the station's curtain shut, placing a barrier between me and the baby.

"Real mature," Casha says. She pulls it back open.

"Please, keep that shut . . . I can't . . . " I back away. *Breathe, Neil. Breathe.*

"He's crying because his dad waited *two whole weeks* to show up," Casha says.

"He's crying because he's an infant," I say.

"Take him. He's yours."

"I don't understand. I mean, you're a . . . machine, so . . . "

"You're going to bring *racism* into this?"

"Whoa!" I put up my hands, shaking my head. "No! I don't . . . how can it be . . . no, listen. I just didn't think . . . "

"Sex equals babies, Neil. *Duh.*"

I remember back to sex ed, Mrs. Pilsner explaining the different ways of getting pregnant: "Women can get pregnant one of two ways. The first is if someone jizzes in her cunt. This is how baby humans are conceived. This is the most common way, but a man can also impregnate a woman by jizzing in her mouth. In such cases she will give birth to a baby tooth."

"What about butts?" I asked. "My dad says he likes to jizz in woman's butts. Can you get a woman pregnant that way?"

Mrs. Pilsner turned to me. "That's the stupidest question I've ever heard," she said. "Of *course* women can't get butt pregnant. Whatever made you think that was possible? Class, laugh at Neil for his stupidity."

The class laughed. "You're a dumbass, Neil!" they jeered. "You're a stupid shit!"

Bobby Denton sprinted across the room from his desk and kicked me in the nuts. "Retard!" he shouted.

I doubled over, clutching my excruciating testes. "What about . . . men?" I gasped through clenched teeth. "Men have mouths, so can they get pregnant?"

"Everyone, keep laughing," Mrs. Pilsner said. "Neil isn't getting it."

Bobby punched me in the back of the head. "Loser!" he bellowed.

My thoughts return to the present.

"Mrs. Pilsner didn't say anything about machines," I say.

"Who's Mrs. Pilsner?" Casha asks.

"She's . . . it doesn't matter."

Casha sighs. "Neil, I have other customers to serve. Hurry up and take your purchased item."

"But it's yours, too, isn't it?"

"*He.* And you *bought* him."

"I mean, biologically . . . "

She throws her hands in the air and gives an

exasperated cry. "What on earth does biology have to do with a *business transaction*?"

"I didn't know it was a fucking transaction, okay? I thought you had sex with me because you wanted to, not because you wanted to *sell* me something! And I didn't know machines could get pregnant!"

She scoffs. "You thought it was because I wanted to? With *you?*"

"No need to be hurtful."

"Hey! Can you hurry it the fuck up?" a man asks. A line is building behind me with him at the front.

"I'm really sorry about this," Casha says. "Could you go to another lane? We'll compensate you for your trouble."

The man grumbles and walks off, other members of the line following. Casha turns off the light and turns back to me. "Listen, Neil. The manager gave instructions for all cashiers to solicit sexual intercourse from customers of the opposite sex. The rise in porn addiction means fewer people are fucking, which means fewer babies are being born, which means fewer consumers. Fewer consumers is bad for our bottom line. It's that simple. I'm sorry you don't understand how the world works, but that's not my fault."

"Well then, call the manager here so I can talk to him!"

"Ugh, fine."

She presses a button on her side of the counter. Minutes pass. I start to wonder if the manager's going to show up.

More minutes pass.

"Is he going to—"

"Hi!"

I jump, yelping. A husky man with a large white handlebar mustache has appeared suddenly next to me.

"How did you . . . there was no one there just . . . "

"What's the problem here?" he asks.

"This asshole won't take the baby he purchased," Casha says.

MY WEIRD NIGHTMARE BABY

"Yes, may I have a refund?" I ask. "It was an accidental purchase, and I don't want it."

"You can't just give it back. It's a baby," the manager says.

"Surely someone who actually *wants* him can have him."

A gunshot rings out. The manager's ear transforms into a mouth and chomps on something; the mouth ejects a spit-covered bullet and turns back into an ear.

"What just happened?" I ask.

"Assassination attempt," he says.

Another shot. Again the ear-mouth catches it and spits it out.

"Oh, will you knock it off!" the manager shouts.

A third shot, but this one from a different direction. There's a cry from above, and a dead man crashes to the street. Shoppers shriek as they leap clear.

"Security got him," the manager says. He turns to me. "Now listen. I can see that you're young, and—"

"Forty-five."

"And you haven't likely given much thought to this."

"Plenty of thought, believe me."

"But as you will no doubt learn, having a child is really quite rewarding. If you don't take him, you will surely come to regret it."

"Yeah, think about it," Casha says. "When you're too old to take care of yourself, who's going to help you?"

"I'll cross that bridge when I come to it."

"Having a child was the best thing that ever happened to me!" shouts a random woman from the street.

"That's great for you, but who are you and who invited you to this discussion?" I ask.

"Where are my grandchildren, Neil?" Mom asks, popping out from behind a shelf in a wheelchair.

"Get lost, Mom!"

The manager lifts the baby off the counter and holds him toward me.

"Please don't," I say.

"Surely you can't say no to this delightful bundle of joy, Sir. These fat little toes? These cherubic cheeks?"

He advances as I continue to back away.

"Why are you backing away?" he asks. "Are you a *baby hater*?"

He thrusts the baby at my chest.

"Please, I—"

A shot. The manager's too distracted to block: His head bursts and blood splatters all over me, over Casha, over the counter, and onto the white tile floor like ketchup on enamel. The baby falls from his arms and strikes the floor head-first. It stops crying.

"Shit!" I scream. "Jesus!"

"You're a cold bastard, Neil," Casha says. "You could have just loved him, like a parent is *supposed* to. But now look. He's dead because you denied him your affection, and you've lost your chance forever. I hope this haunts you for the rest of your life."

Cold. Not the first time I've been called that. I can't always help it—a doctor once told me my emotions are stunted due to the trauma I experienced at such a young age. But am I really the coldest one here?

"*I'm* cold? What about you?" I ask. "You criticize me for failing to love the baby, but you wouldn't even recognize him as your own. You and everyone else, you all talk about how babies are so wonderful, but then you turn around and objectify them, treating them like products. Which is it? Are babies valuable in their own right, or is their value limited to their exploitability as economic assets? It can't be both."

"Pay and leave," Casha says. "Or I'll get the police involved."

Grumbling, I hand her my card and she runs it. She hands it back to me, then presses a button and says, "Can I get a cleanup in aisle 10,405,602?"

CHAPTER FOUR

A CROWD GATHERS at the waterfront, facing a pair of nicely groomed men in posh suits.

"What's going on?" I ask.

"It's a political debate," a woman says. "Didn't you hear? The manager was assassinated yesterday. There's going to be an election."

"Uh, sure. I, uh, heard about that."

The man on the left steps up to a microphone. "If you elect me, there's going to be change," he says.

"Awesome," says a man in assless chaps. "Things suck right now."

The other candidate approaches his microphone. "I also intend to change things," he says.

"Ooh, this is tough," says the assless chaps man.

"I'm gonna vote for the guy on the left. I like his hair," says a full-grown female tooth.

I continue on my way, then nearly trip as my foot hits something on the ground.

"Hey!" complains the man on the ground.

"What are you doing down there?" I ask.

"I'm protesting."

"Protesting what?"

"I don't know, but you'd better stop doing it."

"I see."

The streets are ugly today. Civil unrest oozes like pus from the hole left by the manager's death. Rioters break windows, set fires, cause all manner of mayhem; the police,

understaffed, try but fail to turn the tide. Beating people with their nightsticks, shooting rubber bullets. Sirens blare from all directions.

Dick is watching the news when I arrive at work.

"Hold on," the newscaster says. "I've just received some breaking news."

He must be about to talk about what's happening outside.

"Footage has surfaced of a rather troubling incident," he continues. "And . . . hold on, I've just received word that a victim of the encounter is in the studio today. Welcome, Maria Vance."

A young woman joins the newscaster on screen. I think I recognize her.

"So Maria, you're a new mother," the newscaster says.

"That's right," she says.

"Congratulations."

"Thank you."

"Could you tell us a little bit about what happened last week?"

"I was in the Central Baking District," she says. "Something came up, and I needed someone to watch my baby for a moment."

"Reasonable."

"So I walked up to that young man—Neil, I think it was?"

"Neil Pierson."

What the fuck?

"Yes. I walked up and asked him if he wouldn't mind looking after my baby. And he was very rude to me! It was truly unbelievable. *I* held that baby in my womb all that time. *I* endured hours of painful labor to deliver her. *I* change her diapers and get no sleep because she cries all day and night. I have sacrificed *so* much to give the world the gift of my wonderful child with my wonderful genes. And *this* guy bitches and moans about having to hold her for sixty seconds? Ridiculous!"

"Boohoo lady, you're such a fucking martyr," I say.

MY WEIRD NIGHTMARE BABY

Dick turns to me. "Shit, Neil, this isn't good," he says. "They don't sound like they're happy with you at all."

"Quiet, I'm watching," I say.

"Then what happened?" the newscaster asks.

"Some other mothers walked up," Maria says. "They also needed someone to watch their babies. And this guy . . . "

She lowers her head, shaking slightly.

"It's okay," the newscaster says. "Take your time. I'm sure this traumatized you."

She appears to regain her composure. "It's okay. I can keep going. The other mothers, they asked him to watch their children, and—he kept on being rude. He *hit* one of them. Just punched her, right in the face."

She's crying now. The newscaster puts a hand on her shoulder. "Thank you for your bravery, Maria."

"I didn't punch anyone," I say.

A man in a bear costume walks on screen and takes a seat beside Maria. Neither she nor the newscaster makes any comment.

"That's beary fucked up," the bear man says.

"There does exist footage of the altercation," the newscaster says. "However, due to its disturbing nature, we will not be showing it today. I'm sure it's on the internet somewhere, if you're into watching that sort of thing."

"Fuck Goldilocks," the bear man says. "That bitch drank all my porridge. I'm a bear."

"I wish I could tell you the story ends there, but it doesn't," the newscaster says. "Neil Pierson is apparently the fuckhead who keeps on giving, because yesterday . . . " He produces a water bottle and angrily chugs from it. His face is beet red and getting redder. "Yesterday, this asshole was caught *again* engaging in some goddamn motherfucking *bullshit!*" He pounds the table with his fist. "I'm sorry folks, I'm just awful steamed right now. Get this. Neil Pierson got into a fight with a cashier yesterday over a baby. Guess whose baby? His baby. Because he didn't want it. He even refused to *pay* for it. His own baby!"

"I'd rip him to shreds with my claws," the bear man says. "I'm a bear."

"There is now a warrant out for Neil Pierson's arrest," the newscaster says. "All citizens are advised to be on the lookout for this man, who is described as five foot nine with brown hair and blue eyes. A picture will be on the screen momentarily."

Bastard. I'm six feet.

A picture of a penis appears on the screen.

"Um, no, that's my penis," the newscaster says, blushing. "I'm sorry about that."

A picture of me appears on the screen.

"Neil Pierson is likely to be armed and dangerous. And now, Neil's mother is here to join us on the show."

Mom walks into the frame and sits down.

"Damnit Mom!"

"You should go, Neil," Dick says. "The boss isn't going to like this when he hears about this."

"I've heard about it, and I don't," my boss says.

"Oh. He's behind you," Dick says.

I turn to face the barrel of a flamethrower, aimed at me.

"You're fired, Neil," the boss says.

I dive to the side as flame splooges from the weapon's head, so close I feel the heat. My shoulder hits the floor and pain erupts. Dick is screaming—he didn't move in time from behind me. He screams and screams. It smells like burning Dick.

The boss approaches. "It's over."

In all the chaos, we forgot about Jimbob. He lets out a gleeful squeal from the conveyor several feet away. "I'm going to become dentures at last!" he exclaims.

The boss whirls away from me. "Jimbob, no!"

A terrible cacophony follows. Grinding, crashing, screeching—then silence. The heavy horror of anticipation. Then another horror, more tangible: A tentacle rises above the machines, green and slimy and thick as a tree trunk.

MY WEIRD NIGHTMARE BABY

"Shit!" The boss aims the flamethrower at the tentacle, then appears to realize the folly of it. He throws the weapon aside and flees at a waddling pace to the bathroom. The door slams shut behind him.

The machine has given Jimbob a serious makeover: He looks like a mound of boogers, with liquid shit trickling down the sides. He's got a fuckton of eyes, more eyes than any creature needs, as if nature had an excess of eyes and gave them all to him. Thousands of eyes, all veiny and bloodshot. All of them looking at me.

Fuck.

"Neeeiil," the abomination groans. It's what mucus would sound like if mucus had a sound. "Yooou always pulled me off the machine. You delayed my evolution into dentures. Die."

"Look at yourself, Jimbob! You're not dentures, you're—I don't know what you are, but this can't possibly be what you wanted!"

"I am dentures," Jimbob says.

His tentacle—he has just one—sweeps toward me. I run, ducking under, vaulting over, dodging around machinery. The tentacle is close behind, smashing through everything in its way.

I reach the container where "defective" dentures are collected to be sent to the incinerator. I press the red button and the dentures spill onto the floor. They swarm Jimbob like ants on food. "Brothers and sisters!" he cries. "Why? I am just like you!"

With Jimbob slowed down, I'm able to make it to the exit. I throw open the door and run outside. *Shit, that was close,* I think, panting. *But I should be safe for now.*

"Stop! Put your hands up!"

Dozens of cops stand around the building, guns trained on me. *Fuck. Out of the frying pan and into the fire.* I raise my hands, palms forward to show them I'm not holding anything.

"Don't try anything, baby hater," one shouts. "Or we'll shoot!"

So much for safe.

"What's your relationship to the suspect?" the prosecutor asks.

"I'm his mother."

"Damnit Mom," I whisper.

"Would you say that Neil Pierson is a baby hater?" the prosecutor asks.

"Well, he won't give me grandchildren," she says.

"I'm sorry to hear that. That's my only question."

"Would the defense care to cross-examine this witness?" the judge asks.

"Nah," says my defense attorney. He leans back in his chair and takes a puff of his cigar.

"Take this seriously," I hiss at him.

"Relax," he says.

Next up to the witness stand is a burly, blond-haired man, about six feet tall. I've seen him somewhere before.

"Could you state your name?" the prosecutor asks.

"Bobby Denton," the witness says.

Of course, that's why—that bastard used to bully me in elementary school.

"Tell me about Neil Pierson, Bobby," the prosecutor says. "Is he a baby hater?"

"Well, he called me a fuckhead once," Bobby says.

The prosecutor gasps. "A *fuck*head?"

"Yep. I still haven't gotten over it."

I shoot from my chair, sending the metal legs scraping along the tile floor. Everyone in the room stares at me. "You kicked me in the nuts, asshole! You hit me with a *baseball* bat!"

"Pipe down!" the judge commands.

I return to my seat.

"And then, there was this one time in court, that he called me an asshole," Bobby says.

"Very disturbing stuff," the prosecutor says. "I have no more questions."

"Defense?" The judge asks.

"Nah," says my attorney.

I swivel to face him. "Come on!"

"Relax," he says.

An old man takes the stand and states his name is Robert Jenkins.

"Robert, do you know the defendant, Neil Pierson?"

"Nope, but he looks like a shit," the man says.

"Thank you. No further questions."

"I've never met him in my life!" I protest.

"*Pipe down!*" the judge bellows.

The prosecutor approaches the front of the room and faces the audience. "In closing," he says, "Neil Pierson is a loser and an assbag, and he sucks."

He returns to his seat.

"Defense?" the judge asks.

"Nah," says my attorney.

"*Do your job!*" I scream at him.

"Bring in the manager," the judge says.

A large door opens on the side of the room. The monster that was once Jimbob is wheeled before the court.

Wait. Manager? They put *Jimbob* in charge?

"What is your verdict?" asks the judge.

"Guuuuiiiilty," Jimbob groans.

"Of course he thinks I'm guilty!" I protest. "He's still angry at me for not letting him become . . . whatever he is sooner!"

The judge pounds his gavel. "*Shut. Up.*" He clears his throat. "It's clear, Neil Pierson, that your values are in need of realignment. As such, I sentence you to look after a baby for the next twelve months." He pounds the gavel again, making it official, then adds: "And parenting classes. To make sure you don't *fuck it up.*"

CHAPTER FIVE

A KNOCK AT my apartment door. I answer. It's a deliveryman with a small cage, about the size of a cat carrier.

"Your baby," he says.

The thing in the cage is small and baby-shaped, but it's not like any baby I've ever seen. It has tiny horns and red eyes.

"What's wrong with it?" I ask.

"What do you mean? It's a baby."

"I'm gonna cut you up," the baby says.

The man pushes the cage into my living room and opens it. The baby crawls out and gives me an evil grin. It commences to palm a matchbook from the tabletop and set the rug to a smolder.

"What the hell!" I stomp the rug, putting it out. "Please. I don't want this thing."

"Don't do the crime if you can't do the time," the man says. He leaves and shuts the door. Seconds later, something slams into it. A second strike blows it free of its frame, broken in two. Mom bursts into the room.

"BABY!!!" she howls. Her ravenous eyes scan the room and fall on the demonic infant. "BABY!!!"

"God, Mom, not so loud," I tell her. People are peeking in, wondering what the commotion is.

She picks up the baby. It glares at her, and I'm afraid it's going to hurt her.

"Maybe you should put it down," I say.

MY WEIRD NIGHTMARE BABY

"HE'S SO CHUBBY!!!" she bellows. She swings him around, tosses him in the air and catches him, squeezes him and does a bunch of other stuff you're not supposed to do with a baby. Finally, she puts him down and turns to me. "You know this is only the *first,* right?"

I can't fall asleep. I'm too scared of what the baby will do to me if I do. The bedside lamp's on so I can see him—he's in the corner, holding a steak knife.

"Just sleep," he says.

The light goes out. Frantically, I pull the lamp's chain, to no avail. My failure to pay the electric bill has caught up to me.

Two red eyes stare down from the ceiling.

"*Sleep.*"

The moment I've been dreading arrives: I have to leave the apartment, and I can't leave the baby behind.

Fortunately, I prepared for this. I dress in the hazmat suit I ordered online and open the window. I can't use the door; after getting the broken one replaced, I boarded the new one up so Mom can't come in. She's scratching at the wood on the other side, as she has been for the last two days.

I hoist the baby's stroller through the window and deposit it on the other side. Then, with a deep breath, I lift the baby and put him in the stroller, fighting to keep down bile as I do so. Lastly, I climb through and close the window behind me.

The landlord is waiting for me.

"My *money,* Neil," he says. "I grow tired of this."

"I got fired," I say.

He stomps his foot. "*Excuses* are not payment!"

35

"I'm sorry. I really am."

I push past him and nearly run into another man—tall, lanky, and neatly dressed. He turns to my landlord. "I need my money, Jim."

"I'm sorry," my landlord—Jim—says. "I won't have it until *he*—" he points to me—"pays me."

A woman in a fancy dress and gold jewelry walks up and addresses the lanky man: "Henry, you are two *weeks* overdue on your payment."

"Jim won't pay me!" Henry protests.

"*He* won't pay *me!*" Jim shouts, again pointing at me.

"I lost my damn job, okay?" I say.

The woman looks at me and scoffs. "So *you're* the one gumming up the works," she says. "Miserable parasite."

A gold-painted Rolls Royce Phantom pulls up to the curb and the window rolls down. Inside is an enormous man, easily five hundred pounds, surrounded by stacks upon stacks of hundred-dollar bills. He takes a puff of a cigar, which has a singed hundred wrapped around it.

"Meredith," he says, "I hope work is going well today. Are you meeting your quotas?"

"Er. Yes, sir," she says.

"Good. I hope so."

"*He's* the real parasite," I say. "He's got enough money in there for everyone on this curb."

"And I look forward to not using it to buy the book on socioeconomic theory you're *clearly* working on," the man says. "Get those quotas, Meredith." He slams the door and drives off.

"I think the takeaway is that we're *all* victims here," I say.

"Oh, shut up," Jim says.

Two days after the violence that overtook the city, things have bounced back to normal. The people here are fickle

like that, never sticking with anything for long. Only the shattered windows everywhere serve as reminders that anything happened at all.

I arrive in the infant goods district and flag down a shopping assistant.

"What's with the suit?" she asks.

"I'm into eccentric fashion. Baby formula?"

"Turn on Philips and walk three blocks. Is there a specific kind you're looking for? We have . . . " She looks at a device on her arm. "Six billion, five hundred million, three hundred thousand, nine hundred and fifty-six different kinds."

I blink. "Six . . . billion?"

"Yep."

In the stroller, the baby starts crying. He does this sometimes—acts like a real baby—I think because he knows I hate it.

"Oh, he's so cute," the woman says.

"Is there one kind of food that's better than the others?" I ask.

"Don't know about better, but some of them have side effects."

"Side effects like . . . "

"Pain. Diarrhea. Stuff like that. Just read the labels and you'll see."

"Uh, thanks. What about sleeping pills?"

She gasps. "Sleeping pills for your baby? You're not supposed to—"

"For *me,* obviously."

She examines my drooping eyes and my slumped, weary posture. "Sorry. Nearest pharmacy is on Yalsh Street."

"Thanks."

"If your baby is crying because he needs milk, there's a milk station over there." She points to a black pedestal. It says "milk" on it. I've seen them around but never knew what they were for.

"All right," I say.

I walk over to it. The top opens automatically, revealing a pair of very real-looking tits. I lower the baby's face to the right nipple and he sucks on it. When he's done, I walk away and the top closes. The man behind me steps up, but he doesn't have a baby; gleefully grinning, he begins to fondle the tits. "Ah yeah," he says. "Come to Papa."

Next, I locate the baby food. There're shelves and shelves and shelves of the stuff, as far as the eye can see. I pick up a can. Side effects are listed on the side: Cramping. Temporary blindness. Testicle pain.

"I'll eat your eyeballs," the baby says.

"You know what, you little shit?" I put the food in my shopping basket. "You'll just have to deal with it."

Back at home, I crush up the sleeping pills and mix them in with the food. I put it in a bowl and give it to the baby.

"For you," I say.

"Not hungry," he says.

"You need to eat. If you don't eat, you'll die and they'll blame me."

"The only one who's gonna die is you."

The parenting classes are held in a labyrinthine complex of sterile white corridors. After several wrong turns, I find the room. It reminds me of my schooldays, cheap carpet and cheap desks facing a whiteboard at the front. It evokes memories of teasing and testicle pain.

Five women are already here with their babies, but luckily there's an open seat in the back. I navigate my stroller to it and sit. A sixth woman enters the room and walks to the board. "Hello, ladies," she says. "I'm your teacher, Marin Sylvester. I—" She pauses, looking at me. "You in the back. What's with the suit?"

"I have a contagious disease," I reply. "Very serious. Don't want anyone else to catch it."

MY WEIRD NIGHTMARE BABY

"You must be Neil," she says. "They warned me you'd be trouble. First day, and already you're clowning around." She looks at the rest of the class. "Ladies, this is Neil Pierson. You may have heard about him on the news. He's a *baby hater*."

A chorus of gasps. The women draw their babies close, exchanging whispered gossip: "I heard he's a pedophile." "I heard he killed someone." "I heard he *eats* people."

"Neil," Marin says. "I want to make something clear. I do not want you here. I am sure you do not want to be here, either. Yet we must suffer each other. So I ask of you, *please*, do not make this more difficult than it needs to be."

"Yes, Ma'am," I say.

"Thank you. Next item of business: As I have told you my name, I would like to learn each of yours. Neil we already have the displeasure of knowing. How about the rest of you?"

The five women introduce themselves as Beth, Kima, Natalie, Lisa, and Manuella, and each gives her baby's name as well.

"Excellent," Marin says. "Let's get started, then. I'll ask some questions. What should you do if your baby is crying, and you can't make him or her stop?"

Lisa raises her hand.

"Yes?" Marin says.

"You say 'aww, how cute.' Then you take a video and upload it to social media," Lisa says.

"Yes, that's one thing you can do. But you should also have a list of options to try. Burping the baby, feeding the baby, and so on. In a moment, we'll discuss what should be on this list—

"Excuse me," Manuella says.

"Yes," Marin says.

"Is this before or after my child has cured cancer?" Manuella asks.

"Hold on," Beth says. "*My* child is going to be the one to cure cancer."

"What are you two on about?" Kima asks. "It's obviously going to be mine."

"My child is going to pioneer other planets," Lisa says.

"My child *has* cancer," Natalie says.

The whole room turns to her.

"Wow," Lisa says.

"I'll bet she *smoked* while she was pregnant," Beth whispers.

"Let's get back on track, ladies," Marin says. "Next question: What do you do when your baby poops his or her diaper, and you forgot to pick up more diapers at the store?"

Lisa raises her hand and Marin calls on her.

"You say 'aww, how cute.' Then you take a video and upload it to social media," Lisa says.

"Is this before or after my child has solved the global pollution problem?" Manuella asks.

"Again with you?" Beth snaps. "*My* child is—"

"Ladies, ladies! Please, let's not get sidetracked," Marin says.

"I have a question," I say.

Marin sighs. "Fine. Go ahead."

"Can you give me advice on how I can get some goddamn sleep when my baby is making noise at all hours of the night?"

Lisa turns to me and says, 'You say 'aww, how cute.' Then you take a video and upload it—"

"Can I get a *helpful* answer?"

"Excuse me?" Marin says. "We're all trying to help each other here."

"Okay, but—"

"You forfeited your right to sleep when you signed up to help raise the next generation. This is about them. Not *you*. But I wouldn't expect someone as selfish as you to understand that."

"Okay. Whatever."

The baby grins at me. "I'll grind you up. I'll make you

into chili," he whispers, too quietly for anyone else to hear.

"I have one more question," I say.

"What?" Marin shouts, smacking the whiteboard. "What horseshit do you have to disrupt the class with now? Oh! Maybe you're going to complain about how you have to *watch* the baby instead of sitting around sucking your own dick like you're no doubt used to! Am I right?"

"Actually, I was wondering how I can get him to stop threatening to kill me."

She stares at me. "What on *earth* are you talking about?"

"Just listen," I say.

I hold the baby up so everyone can hear.

"I'm gonna rip your fucking guts out," he says.

The women once again gasp in unison.

"*What* did he just say?" Marin asks.

"That's what I'm talking about."

"You taught your baby to *curse*?" Manuella asks.

"No, I didn't teach him anything—"

"I assure you, Neil, the court will hear of this," Marin says.

"Fine. I'm sorry. I won't ask for help on anything."

"Thank you."

The baby is gone.

"Another question," Marin says. "Suppose you've just had your tenth child, and . . . "

I spot him. He's by Manuella's desk, and I don't know how, but he's got a knife.

"Watch out!" I shout.

He pulls Manuella's baby off her and stabs it in the neck. Then he's back in my lap and the baby's soaking in a pool of its own juices on the floor, making little choking sounds.

"Oh my God! My baby!" Manuella screams.

Lisa yells, "Quick, take a picture and—"

"He's *dead!*"

"Oh. Oh no," Marin says. "Um . . . well, this happens sometimes. Not all babies will make it."

"Was it a miscarriage?" Kima asks.

"I'll bet she *smoked* while she was pregnant," Beth whispers.

CHAPTER SIX

"**I**'ll **burn you** alive," the baby says.

"I've had enough of you," I say. "I don't care what they do to me. You're a murderer."

"Drown in feces," he says.

I put my hands around his neck. He doesn't try to stop me. I squeeze until he's no longer breathing.

Come nighttime, I bundle him in cloth and carry him to the river. The air is freezing and homeless are gathered at fires on the waterfront, fighting to stay warm. They pay no heed to me or the bundle in my arms.

I drop the baby, weighted down by rocks, into the water. He slowly sinks out of sight.

The interviewer sits in a gold-plated chair, in front of a lavish cocobolo desk. I take a seat in the plastic green folding chair opposite her.

"Why do you want this job?" she asks.

I look out her office window to the factory floor below. It's the kind of oppressive industrial hellscape I know all too well—sweaty, grime-coated workers toiling away at machines that may delimb them at any moment. I don't want to return to this. But you're not supposed to say that. You're supposed to pretend you *like* getting bitten by dentures every day, or you can forget about money to feed yourself.

"Well?" she says. "I'm waiting."

I've got to come up with something. I continue to scan the factory and see that some workers are fondling what appear to be giant mounds of red gelatin.

"I like gelatin," I say.

She cocks her head. "You like *gelatin*?"

"Yeah."

"Sir, we make defibrillators."

"Oh."

"You didn't *know* we make defibrillators?"

"I, uh, of course I did."

"Do you even know what a defibrillator *is*?"

"It's . . . uh . . . "

"Goodbye, sir."

"Just one question."

She sighs. "Fine."

"Can I ask you why the name of your company is "Jonesy's Burgers?"

"*Goodbye.*"

The office is painted a sickening lime green and smells like cheese. I sit down on a seat that resembles an oversize sandwich.

"Eggs?" the interviewer asks. His head is shaped roughly like a bowling ball and his nose is the size of a small orange.

"Uh, sorry. Did you say eggs?"

He stands and walks to my side. "Eggs?" He sniffs my hair. "Eggs?" He lifts my arm and sniffs the pit.

"Why are you sniffing me?" I ask.

"I'm sorry," he says. "I can't give you this job."

"What? But you haven't even—"

He lifts the bottom of my shirt to his nose and blows, loud as a tuba. Snot guzzles out and just keeps coming— must be a liter at least. Finally, he lets go of my mucus-soaked shirt. "Interview's over," he says.

MY WEIRD NIGHTMARE BABY

"I really don't know what's going on here."

"Get the fuck out."

"One last question," the interviewer says. "I'm going to show you a picture of my penis, and I want you to tell me what you think."

He winks and begins to unbutton his shirt. He already removed his pants earlier in the interview and is wearing a leopard-skin speedo.

"I'm uncomfortable with where this interview is going," I say.

"Uncomfortable? How so?"

"It's the way you keep hitting on me. I'm sorry, but I'm not interested."

"*Hitting* on you? Preposterous! That would be highly unethical!"

He stands from his chair and walks to the fridge at the far side of the room. He removes a bottle of wine and steps into a hot tub next to the fridge. "Join me," he says.

"I don't know how you could make this *any* more suggestive."

"Any more talk like that and the interview's over," he says. "Now, are you going to look at my dick or not?"

"Whatever. Let me see it."

He holds up a blank piece of paper. "What do you think?"

"Uh . . . sorry. Is that the right picture?" I ask.

"Of course it is."

"But there's nothing on the paper."

"What . . . what do you mean there's nothing . . . " He looks at the paper. "This is my penis. It's right here."

"I'm sorry, I . . . "

Tears fill his eyes. Next thing I know, he's sobbing into his hands. "Nothing . . . you said it's nothing . . . "

A hand grabs my shoulder. I'm spun face-to-face with

a musclebound, seven-foot-tall Hispanic man. "What did you do?" he demands. "Why's the boss crying?"

"I . . . " I gulp. This guy could make me into paste with just his foot. "I . . . "

The interviewer blubbers, "He, he . . . he said that my penis is *nothing*!"

The giant's grip on my shoulder tightens.

"Shit. That hurts," I say.

Fury burns in his eyes. "You piece of shit. He's *very* sensitive about his penis size."

"You expect me to have been able to know that?"

He launches me into the wall with a shove. "Just get the fuck out of here. If I ever see you again, I'll kill you."

"I see that you have a baby," the interviewer says.

"Me?" I laugh. "Nah. Babies aren't really my thing."

He types something on his computer. "Baby hater. Interesting."

"No! Is there *any*one in the world who understands the distinction?"

"If you don't have a baby," he says, "Then what's that?"

He points to something behind me. *What? What's back there?* Cold explodes through my veins the second I turn to look. The baby is sitting next to the door. "Miss me?" he asks.

"How in the . . . "

"Excuse me. The interview?"

"Right." I turn back to the interviewer. "Um . . . sorry, what was the question?"

"I haven't asked a question yet."

"Oh. Okay."

I can feel the baby staring at me.

"I don't like employees with babies. Always begging for leave so they can watch their kids. Is that gonna be a problem with you?"

MY WEIRD NIGHTMARE BABY

"No."

"And you're not gonna fucking quit so you can go and start a large family, like my last six employees?"

"Definitely not. I need the money, so . . . "

He frowns. "Money. It's just about the money for you."

"I just mean I'm not going to do any of that stuff you apparently think I'm going to do. I need to work—I *want* to work. I want to work *here*. Your company does . . . stuff with feces? Is that right? That's like my dream job. Love feces."

"Hmm." He strokes his beard and taps his desk. "Well. I'm sorry."

"Sorry?"

"Can't hire you. I don't want to risk the possibility that you'll get pregnant again—pregnant people are terrible workers."

"Uh . . . you realize I'm a man, right?"

"What difference does that make?"

Mrs. Pilsner would have loved this guy. "Men can't *get* pregnant."

He shrugs. "Don't believe you. Sounds like you're just trying to convince me to hire you. Not gonna work."

"You're an idiot."

"And you're leaving my office."

"How are you still alive?" I ask the baby.

He smiles, then shits himself.

The unemployment office is on Hawken Street, two miles from my apartment. Getting there means passing through the produce district, where sprinklers spray me with a fine mist as I walk through towering rows of vegetables. I then enter the mall district, a colossal complex of buildings

housing miles upon miles of storefronts. As usual, the area is packed to the brim with people—I avoid coming here when I can help it.

"Hey, no butting in line," a man says.

Upon closer inspection, some members of the crowd have formed a line, which snakes into the distance and disappears around a corner.

"Sorry, I'm just trying to get to the unemployment office," I say.

"Are you kidding me?" he snaps. "You think this is the line for the unemployment office? Do I *look* like a freeloader to you?"

"Er, no," I say. How could this be the line? The office is still a mile away. "I'm just gonna go. Have a nice day."

"Hey. Eat shit. I'm not just gonna let you walk off after insulting me."

"Calm down, okay?"

He jabs my chest with his finger. "I *work* for a living."

"Good for you."

He takes out his wallet. "Here's my wallet. Go on, take it. You might as well. Do you know how much of my tax money goes to supporting you useless fucks?"

"Do *you*?"

"Whatever, man. You know what? Forget it. I'm above this." He crosses his arms and turns away.

"Okay," I say.

He snaps back to face me. "If it'll make you leave, asshole, I'll tell you where to go. *That's* the loser line over there." He points to an equally long line running parallel to his. *Shit. I guess it's this long after all. Gonna be here a while.*

I join the line behind a tall blonde woman. "What's that other line for?" I ask her.

"Some fancy new gadget," she says. "I plan to buy it just as soon as I get my unemployment money."

"You don't know what it is?"

"I know it's popular, and that's all I need."

MY WEIRD NIGHTMARE BABY

A man steps up behind me. He's got a wagon stroller with four infants in it.

"This is the line for unemployment?" he asks.

"I guess so," I say.

"I can't believe this," he says. "There never used to be lines like this."

A woman walks up. She also has four infants in a stroller, and one in a carrier on her back. "Is this the line, Phil?" she asks.

"I'm afraid so, sweetie," the man says.

A boy joins them; he can't be older than ten. He's pushing a double stroller, two babies. Three girls, I'd guess the five-to-seven age range, come up behind him with a double stroller each.

"These are all your kids?" I ask.

"Yep!" the mother says cheerfully.

Phil's still fuming. "It's just absurd," he says. "Absolutely absurd. Where are all these people *coming* from? I'm telling you, Margaret, the lines never used to be this long! And the *traffic* these days . . . "

"I suppose it's just people coming in from elsewhere," Margaret says.

"That's right," he says. "It's all those damned *immigrants*. The black ones and the yellow ones and the red ones and the green ones."

"Green?" I say.

"And the purple ones. It's like a goddamn rainbow. They're destroying our culture!"

"*That*, we can agree on," says Mr. "Do-I-look-like-a-freeloader" from the other line.

I look at their kids. "Right. Couldn't be any other reason for the population increase."

"Definitely," he says. "Glad I'm not the only one who sees it."

A woman's voice blares over the intercom, "Attention everyone. At the behest of Lord Dentures, the unemployment office is now permanently closed. We apologize for the inconvenience."

"What?" Phil says. "That can't be. It must be a joke." Terror is written plainly on his face. "It is . . . isn't it?"

"This is not a joke. Again, we apologize for any inconvenience," the woman says.

"What are we going to do?" Margaret asks. "We can't afford to support our children!"

"Uh, get a job?" Not-a-freeloader says. "Like, wow. Crazy concept, right? Just . . . don't be lazy! How revolutionary!" His phone rings, and he answers it. "Hello?" His expression shifts from passive to angry. "What? What do you mean, I'm fired?"

Margaret's on her knees, shaking with heavy, choking sobs. "We're done for," she moans. "We're done for."

Phil takes her into his arms. "I'm sorry. We did our best."

"I never thought it would come to this," she says.

"Maybe in the next world, things will be better," Phil says.

He bends to the side of his wagon stroller and comes up with a shotgun. *Blam.* Margaret's brains exit her head. *Blam.* Into his skull. They collapse atop each other like lovers. Their children begin to cry. The younger ones because their ears hurt from the blasts; the older because they have some sense of what's happened, even if it's not sunk in yet. "Mommy! Daddy!" they scream as they rush to their parents' sides. Soon they'll understand that Mommy and Daddy won't be getting up again.

Mr. I'm-not-a-freeloader calmly approaches. He picks up the shotgun and puts one end on the ground and the other in his mouth. *Blam.*

Sirens in the distance, fast approaching. An all too normal sound.

CHAPTER SEVEN

IT'S FRIDAY NIGHT and I go to Mackey's, prepared to wash away the week's events in drink. As usual, Nick and Levi are both there.

"You look lousy," Levi says.

Mackey hands me my whiskey and I take a swig. "Yeah. They gave me this weird kid to watch."

"Oh, right," Nick says.

"And I can't get a job."

"Rough," Levi says.

Nick stands up. "I gotta hit the shitter. You know how it is with Mackey's food, always causing diarrhea."

"And I'm damn proud of it," Mackey says.

Nick leaves, and something moves behind Levi's stool. It's the baby.

"Levi, you're a fucker," the baby says, in a perfect imitation of my voice.

Levi slams his drink down and stares at me. "*What* did you just say?"

"It wasn't me," I say. "Look behind you. It's my weird nightmare baby. It keeps following me around."

"Piece of shit," the baby says. "I fucked your mother."

Levi bursts off his stool. He grabs my arm and squeezes so hard it hurts. "I am not. And my mother's not a fucking slut. She's *dead*."

"It's the baby, Levi."

His fist plows into the side of my face, knocking me to the floor.

"Fuck you, Neil. *Fuck* you. You just ended ten years of friendship."

"Hey look, a bar fight!" someone shouts. "Let's watch!"

A crowd gathers. I rub my smarting cheek and stand up. "Go away, it's none of your business," I say.

"Your sister's pussy is the best," the baby says.

A man hops forward on a pogo stick and dismounts. "Did you just imply you *fucked* my sister?" he asks.

"No," I say.

He swings the pogo stick at my shoulder.

"Ow!" I shriek.

"Eat a salad, tubby," says the baby.

"Asshole!" A fat man barrels forward from the back of the crowd and kicks me in the nuts.

"Yeowch!" yells the baby. "Right in the juevos!"

I drop to my knees, clutching my balls, bent forward as if genuflecting to my aggressors.

"Please," I beg the baby. "Please, be quiet."

"Faggot," says the baby.

A woman's fist *crunches* into my nose. I howl at pain so intense it makes my other pains irrelevant. Blood streams from my nostrils down my neck and onto my shirt.

"You piece of shit," she says and spits in my eye.

"She got him good," someone remarks. The crowd disperses, their thirst for violence apparently sated.

"Mackey," I croak.

"What's up?" he asks.

I raise a finger. "Another drink, please," I say, and collapse on the floor.

"You're cut off," Mackey says.

The world goes dark.

"Shit, man. I can't believe all that happened while I was in the bathroom," Nick says. I'm in a hospital bed, hooked up to a network of cords and tubes. A heart monitor beeps

next to me. "And Levi just up and dumping you like that? Crazy. What an asshole."

"Thanks, Nick. You're a good guy."

"Your heart's doing great," says the heart monitor, a cyborg with one mechanical hand attached to my wrist. "I'll give you another update in a minute or so."

"We're kind of trying to have a conversation here," Nick says.

"And I'm trying to let you know if this guy's about to have a heart attack," the heart monitor says.

"I don't think that's very likely," I say.

"Oh yeah? Just look at the kind of *food* you eat."

He points to the gooey green glop on a tray beside me. Whatever it is, it's moving.

"I haven't eaten any of that," I say.

"Whatever you say," the heart monitor says. "Your heart's doing great, by the way."

Nick puts his hand on my arm. "Listen," he says. "I'm not gonna be like Levi. I'll stick by you no matter what, that's a promise."

"Thanks, man," I say.

"You're an ass, Nick," the baby says from underneath the bed.

"Holy *shit,* Neil," Nick says.

"Nick, I just explained all this to you. It's the baby."

"You're a dick, Neil," Nick says. He storms to the exit, stops, turns, and glares at me. "Kill yourself."

He leaves.

"Tough break," the heart monitor says. "But hey, your heart's still good."

"You're a hunk of junk," says the baby.

"You deserve a heart attack," the heart monitor says.

I stand on the bridge, looking down at the toxic New Mississippi water. If the fall doesn't kill me, that water will cook me alive.

My brain screams at me not to do it.

"Go away, survival instinct. Maybe you didn't catch the memo, but my friends have all left me. I'm alone. Just let me do what I need to do."

I close my eyes.

"Goodbye, cruel world," I whisper. I prepare to jump, and pause. "No, I can't go out on that. Too cliché."

"Try 'yippee ki yay, motherfucker,'" a passerby suggests.

Yeah, that might work. I consider it for a moment.

"Fuck this," I say, and jump. It'll have to do.

I'm falling.

Falling.

Falling.

Falling . . .

Awful lot of falling for such a short drop. I open my eyes.

I'm in a net, extending from the side of a police hovercar. The disgruntled hirsute officer floats the car to the bridge and deposits me there.

"I'm in a generous mood today," he says. "Ordinarily there's a fine for this sort of thing. Don't let me catch you trying it again."

I didn't think it would happen, but I've found someone on lovebird.com. Her name's Heather, and she likes meat. I *also* like meat. It's a match made in heaven.

To think that only a couple days ago, I tried to kill myself. Everything's going to change for the better now.

The meatup is arranged to take place at a restaurant called Meat. Meat's all there is on the menu. I dress, shower, and put on my nicest cologne, then head over.

The restaurant's exterior is painted the color of a

cooked steak, but inside the walls are pink, just like a steak's center. Dozens of pictures of meat line the walls, depicting everything from pork chops to filet mignon. The wait staff are dressed as chicken wings and t-bone steaks.

My date's at a table near the wall, drinking a meatshake. I approach her. "Hi, are you—"

The words die on my lips. It's Clive, the butcher from the meat wall. He's got a wig on, but he hasn't shaved. I'd recognize him anywhere.

Thankfully, he's focused on his shake and hasn't noticed me yet. I duck beneath the nearest table, where a woman is seated.

"What are you doing?" she asks.

I whisper for her to be quiet.

She glares down at me. "I'll tell the waiter."

"Something the matter, ma'am?" the waiter asks.

"Yes, there's a man under my table."

He lifts the tablecloth and sees me. "Sir, what are you—"

I burst out from under the table and slam into him. The tray he's holding flies from his hands, showering liquefied meat. I run.

As I swipe my key card to enter my apartment building, someone grabs me from behind. A rag is shoved in front of my mouth, and the world goes dark.

Clive's face is the first thing to greet me when I wake. I try to move my arms and legs and can't; I'm tied to a chair.

His whole house is raw meat: The walls are meat, the floor is meat, the bed is meat. The floor squelches beneath the legs of my chair as I struggle to break free.

"Clive, what the hell," I say.

"I missed you at the restaurant, Neil," he says.

"Something came up."

"Something came up? Is that why you hid under a table and ran?"

Damn. I hoped he hadn't seen me.

"You're kidnapping me because I stood you up?" I ask.

"I thought we *had* something," he says. "We both like meat."

"You know, Clive, when I think about it, that's not really enough to base a relationship on."

He punches me in the stomach. "You piece of shit!"

"Clive," I wheeze, the breath knocked out of me. "It's a misunderstanding. I didn't know it was *you*."

"You didn't *know*? How could you possibly not know?"

"Your profile picture showed a busty, black-haired woman! You don't look like that at all!"

Clive walks to a curtain at the side of the room. He pulls it open, revealing a bathtub full of bubbles.

"No," I say.

"It's the most expensive bubble bath liquid I could find. The best."

"I'm not *gay*."

"I had everything prepared. Candles. The bath. I got *new sheets*. Tonight was supposed to be romantic."

"Clive—"

He pulls out a pistol and thrusts the barrel to my forehead.

"Shit!" I shout. "Clive, no!"

"Get in the tub, Neil! Get in the *fucking tub*!"

"You have to untie me first."

He nods and takes a knife off the table, with which he cuts the rope. I stand and walk to the tub, pointedly aware of the cold metal gun barrel pressed to the small of my back.

"No," Clive says. "No. Not like this. Not if you don't want me."

The gun leaves my back. A shot, then silence just as deafening. I lift my leg from the tub and look despite knowing what I'll see.

Clive is meat.

The next night, I guzzle down half a bottle of cleaning detergent. I lose consciousness shortly after, and wake up in a bright room.

"Oh shit," I say. "There's an afterlife."

"Your heart's still fine," the heart monitor says. "Not that I care, you wretched gizzard."

Oh. It's the hospital again. A nurse enters the room.

"Since this is your second time here in just a few days, might I recommend signing up for our frequent visitors' program? You can acquire points and get discounts on future visits."

"I drank half a bottle of detergent," I say. "I ought to be dead."

"If only," the heart monitor says.

"They removed all the harmful chemicals from that stuff years ago," the nurse says. "Barely even works for cleaning anymore. But it stops morons like you from offing yourselves with it."

"Oh. Why'd I fall unconscious, then?"

"Exhaustion."

That part makes sense, at least. I feel more rested—but not less miserable.

The hairy officer I met at the bridge comes into the room behind her. He shakes his head. "How disappointing. I gave you a second chance, and you blew it."

He hands me a slip of paper. It's a fine—five thousand dollars, to be paid in full within a week. The alternative: prison.

"Get your life together," the officer says.

I take a seat on the frayed red couch. The room is small, populated only by the couch, a chair, and a cluttered

mahogany desk. A painting hangs on the wall, depicting a man being eaten alive by crocodiles in baggy orange pants.

"Do you like it?" asks Doctor Lecker, the therapist. He's bald, broad, and bespectacled.

"Not particularly."

I force myself not to look at it.

Lecker picks up a yellow notepad off his desk and leafs through it. "Ah. Here we are. Suicide attempt," he says. "Cleaning detergent."

I stare at my hands, ashamed to look him in the eye. "Yep. That's the gist of it."

"Okay. Gonna fire off a couple of suggestions," he says.

"All right."

"Number one is obvious. Have a baby. Helps everyone."

"Already have one."

Lecker adjusts his glasses. "You have a baby. And you tried to *kill* yourself."

"Yes."

"Neil, you are aware that babies need their parents to survive."

"You don't know this baby. He'd be just fine."

He sighs. "It's a *baby*."

"Honestly? That's debatable."

"What's your relationship with your family like?" he asks.

"My dad's dead. Mom and I don't get along."

"Why's that?"

"Ever since I got old enough to find a woman and raise a family, she's followed me around, pressuring me to have babies," I say. "She knows I'm scared of babies because babies killed my dad, but in spite of that, she never leaves me alone. I think it's because she was pregnant when my dad died, but it turned out to be a miscarriage. She never got the second baby she wanted from him, so . . ."

"So you also hate your mother."

"No!"

He jots something down on his notepad. "I've made a note: Likely to be a sociopath."

"Sociopath?"

"Absolutely. Let's move on. Suggestion number two—work harder. How many hours a week do you work right now?"

"None."

He scribbles something down. "I've written 'parasite'," he says.

"I was fired!"

"So then next time, don't suck at your job."

"Listen. I'm *depressed,* okay? Don't you have any way to help me with that?"

"You can't be depressed."

"Of course I can be. I am."

"No you're not. They put chemicals in the drinking water nowadays to suppress emotion. Sadness, happiness—all things of the past, at least as we once understood them. Only fear of death, desire for sex, and love of babies has been left intact, for obvious reasons. And anger. That one's like a cockroach, refusing to be stamped out."

"That's nonsense."

"Believe what you want. It's true."

"But . . . "

The possibility *did* make a certain kind of sense. It would explain a thing or two. And I wouldn't put it past "they"—whichever body of power Lecker was referring to—to do something like that.

"If nobody has any emotion, the diagnosis of 'sociopath' has no meaning," I say. "Or does it just mean what you want it to?"

"How do you know what a sociopath is or isn't?" he asks.

"Internet."

"Anybody can put stuff on there. I'm a *therapist.*"

"Well, that's what people call you, at any rate."

"Here's my diagnosis. Aside from being a sociopath, you're an entitled brat who thinks the world should revolve around you. Stop playing the victim. Lay off the martyr complex and *contribute* something. The moment you pull your head from your ass and give something *back* to society for a change, your so-called 'depression' will disappear."

I stare at him. "You're shitting me."

"Our meeting time is up. I'll send you the bill."

There's an eviction notice on my door when I return to my apartment. I try the key in the door and it doesn't work.

"You're not getting in there," the landlord says.

"My stuff's in there."

"Nope. Gone. Sold."

"But . . ."

"You dug your own grave." He shrugs and turns away. "Good luck."

CHAPTER EIGHT

THE SMOGGY AIR looks and smells like a toilet after a night of too much drink. I can feel its oily texture on my skin, in my nose, and at the back of my throat.

In the shadow of the city's factory district lies a world most will never see. The sprawling mass of haphazardly built tents looks, at first, to be a dump, but it's not; people live here. They come here because there's no other place for them to go. They're castoffs, washed away from society by the weathering forces of economic strife; I'm one of them now.

A mother washes laundry in a bucket while her children play in the dirt. Three grizzled men in metal folding chairs drink whiskey as they play with a tattered deck of cards. An elderly man reclines against a post, playing a soulful tune on a harmonica. Multiple eyes both wary and weary follow my every step. I'm one of them, but at the same time, I'm not.

It's not all tents. Some people have built structures out of other materials and objects. Many are unusual: there's a house made of toys, another made of animal bones latched together with wire. One tent is surrounded by surreal humanoid sculptures that I swear are made of dried feces, if the smell and flies are any indication. Even though these people have nearly nothing—no, more likely because they have nearly nothing—they've worked to infuse their spaces with pieces of themselves. These monuments to the ego protect them from losing the last thing they have left: their identities.

I approach the card-playing men. "Excuse me," I say. "Is there any open space around here? Somewhere I can set up for a bit?"

They ignore me. I continue on.

A pair of kids run up to me, a boy and a girl. "Hey mister. Do you got any money?" the girl asks.

"Why would I be here if I have any money?" I ask.

"'You gotta have money. You look nice," her brother says.

He's right; my clothes are clean and intact, no rips or holes. My hair is neatly combed. I must stick out like an elephant in a strip club.

"Sorry," I say. "You're out of luck."

They return to their mother, who scowls at me. She must think I'm lying. I turn onto another street similarly lined with tents.

"Turn around," a man says in a growly, "I'd-better-do-the-opposite-and-run" kind of voice. I gulp, picking up my pace.

"*Turn. Around.*"

Or get hurt, the tone implies. I oblige. It's the card-playing men. They don't look like they're here to play nice.

"Er . . . may I help you?" I ask. I'm shaking, legs feel like they're turning to mush.

"Hey buddy," Growly Voice says. He's lanky and gaunt. "You lost?"

"No," I say.

"Really. Doesn't seem like your part of town," says the gangly man with a red, bushy beard on Growly's right.

"I don't have a part of town anymore."

"So you're saying you belong here," Growly says.

"Exactly. I lost my home. We're in the same boat."

"Same boat, huh?" It's the third man, who's teapot-shaped. "Funny. I see clean clothes. What you got in your pocket there? Cell phone, wallet? You're not like us."

"You say same boat?" Redbeard says. "This is our boat. We didn't invite you on board."

MY WEIRD NIGHTMARE BABY

"Hey, don't you feel like you've seen this guy somewhere before?" Teapot says.

"What do you mean?" Growly asks.

"Like, in the paper."

"Holy shit, you're right. He's that baby hater," Redbeard says.

"That makes this a lot easier for us," Growly says. "Nobody will care if this guy disappears."

"You hear that?" Redbeard says. "You're about to be in the paper again. Obits this time."

I hear the snick of a blade released from its socket. Growly takes a step forward, knife glimmering in his hand.

"Hey, please, can't we work this out?" I ask.

"You shouldn't have come here," Growly says.

"Please. I don't want to die."

I don't?

That's right, I don't. Sometimes you think you want something until it's offered to you. I thought I wanted to die; now, death knocks at my door and my pants verge on being creamed.

Growly takes another step. Another. He grins; he's drawing it out, playing with me. I'm frozen. That knife's about to be in me, and I guess my body's decided to just let it happen.

Another step . . .

He screams. The baby's on his neck—its claws are *in* his neck. He geysers blood into the air, a human fountain.

"Fuck!" screams Redbeard. "*Fuck!*"

They run. The baby shoots twin red lasers from its eyes, bisecting the men, guts and bones splattering in a burst of gore.

The baby smiles at me.

"You . . . saved my life," I say.

"Only I get to kill you," he says.

For the first time, I notice there's an audience. Four people are watching; their eyes reveal both fear and respect.

"Spread the word," I tell them. "Don't fuck with me. Or . . . " I gesture to the carnage in front of me. "This is what happens."

"Dude." A man approaches. "That was . . . that was totally *nuts*."

"It was all the baby," I say. "I didn't do a thing."

"He's yours, though, isn't he?"

"He just kind of follows me . . . actually, yeah. He's mine."

"Sick. Listen, are you looking for work? I'm Connor. Come by my tent sometime. It's that red one there."

"I'll come right now," I say.

5:30 p.m. The Target will drive under the Velway Bridge in a black sedan. Kill him.

He arrives not a second late. I watch him turn the corner at the end of the street and approach the bridge.

"Baby," I say.

A flash of red—his lasers—and the car explodes. Tires, metal, and glass go everywhere. A twisting, writhing pyre rises, blasting me with heat. I back away. The baby returns to my side.

"Done," he says.

"Good work," Connor says. I doubt that's his real name. "Go to that hot dog place on Fenson Avenue at seven. There'll be a man in a red and yellow hoodie—he'll give you the cash."

"If you're part of an operation like this, why are you living *here?*" I ask him.

"Low profile," he says. "Plus, I *like* it here."

I find the man in the hoodie at Raw Dog, as Connor said. "Hey," I say to him.

MY WEIRD NIGHTMARE BABY

"Fuck off, fruitcake," he says.

"Huh?"

He stands and walks off, leaving his to-go container. I open it and peek inside. "Holy—" I lower my voice to a whisper. "Holy *shit*. This much?"

I carry the container to the trash can and, making sure no one's watching, stuff the money into my pockets and toss the rest.

"Baby," I say, "This line of work might be just right for us."

"Here is your duck confit, sir," the waiter says, placing the dish on the table in front of me. "As you requested, the chef has sprinkled it with flakes of edible gold. And here, as you also requested, is a bottle of the most expensive wine we have to offer."

"Thank you," I tell him. "You may go now."

He gives a small bow and leaves the room. I rest my dirty feet on the table's silk covering and lean back with a contented sigh. "Baby," I say, "this is the life."

It's been five months since we started the hitman job, and as it turns out, crime *does* pay. The baby and I have recently moved into an upscale apartment downtown, and for tonight, I've rented out the finest restaurant in the city. He's in the seat next to me, staring blankly across the room. He hasn't aged a day—he still looks as if he came out of the womb last week.

At the front of the room is a wooden stage, where musicians and other entertainers sometimes perform. My former landlord, Jim, is there, attempting to juggle a trio of juggling balls. He's doing a piss-poor job, though, and keeps dropping them.

"Boo!" I shout.

"This is humiliating, Neil," he says.

"Hey, cheer up," I say. "At least I'm finally paying you."

I lift a piece of the duck confit to my mouth with a fork and take a bite. "Wow," I say. "This is excellent stuff. Hey, waiter!"

My waiter returns to the table. "Yes, sir?"

"Where's that shoe shiner I asked for?"

"He should be here any minute, sir."

"Thank you."

Two minutes later, the shoe shiner arrives. I recognize him right away—it's the fat man who visited my apartment in the gold Rolls Royce, surrounded by piles of money.

"Holy shit," I say.

He scowls. "Oh. I remember you."

"I can't believe it. How'd a guy like you end up with *this* job?"

"Shut up."

I present my right shoe to him. "Get shining."

He kneels and begins to polish the leather with a cloth. "Am I the only one seeing the hypocrisy here?"

"What hypocrisy?" I ask.

"You were whining about the rich exploiting people. Now look at you."

"Oh, come on. That's totally different."

"*How*?"

"He's right, Neil," Jim says. "You're acting like a pompous ass."

"Keep juggling," I say. "And it's different because my whole life has been shit. I've *earned* a break."

"Everyone's life is shit," Jim says. "You're just being an entitled brat."

"You won't be able to hold onto this life," the fat man says. "Look at what happened to me. Sooner or later, this society will chew you up and spit you out, and you'll be right back where you started."

"Not gonna happen to me," I say.

"Of course you think that," he says.

Outside, a fight breaks out. Mom and the bodyguard I hired are shouting at each other.

"What's going on?" the fat man asks.

"It's my mom. She wants to get in here, but I told the guard at the door not to let her."

"Your own mother?" Jim says. "What is wrong with you?"

"Shut up. You don't know what she's like."

"My mother's dead," the fat man says. "Do you know how badly I wish I could spend even another *second* with her? But you won't even let your mother join you for dinner. You make me sick."

"You're really not one to talk, okay? But fine. You know what, you're right. She's family. I should spend a little time with her every now and then." I turn to the door. "Hey! It's all right, let her in!"

Mom enters the room. I press a button beneath the table, and a trapdoor opens in the floor beneath her. She falls, and the door swings shut, shutting out her screams.

"What did you just do?" Jim shouts.

"I requested that trapdoor be installed just for that reason," I said. "Great, huh?" I take a bite of the duck confit. "You know, before now, I didn't know food this good even existed." I swallow and pick up another piece.

"You're a sociopath!" the fat man shouts.

My hand halts partway to my mouth. The duck slides off the fork and plops onto the floor. I glare at the fat man. "I am *not*," I snarl. I've had enough of these two and their insults. "Baby?"

"Baby? You haven't even named him yet?" Jim asks.

"Kill them," I say.

"Wait, what the fu—"

Jim doesn't finish. Lasers zap him into red mist and chunks, splattering the wall behind like a mural. The fat man shrieks and tries to run, or waddle, away—*Zap*. He dies in a fashion equally spectacular to his partner on stage.

"Dead," the baby says, grinning at his handiwork.

"Yes. Very," I say.

I take a sip of wine and think about what the fat man

said. Perhaps it *is* odd I haven't named the baby yet, given the relationship we've formed over the last few months.

"Baby, what should I call you?" I ask.

"I'll torture you," he says. "I'll hook a car battery to your nipples to shock you. I'll waterboard you."

"No, those aren't very good suggestions," I reply. "I was thinking more like . . . Neil 2.0?"

He glares. "I was thinking of putting you on a Judas cradle."

"What's a—never mind, I'm sure it's something horrible. I take it you don't like that one? Okay, what about . . . " I think about it. "Okay, I've got it. You're gonna be Lazarus, 'cause you shoot lasers."

"Tooth extraction without anesthetic," he says.

"Cool, Lazarus it is." I finish my wine glass and lean back. "Yep, we make a great team, don't we?"

I smile as I survey the carnage around me. All this money, this power . . . I can do whatever I want. No one can stop me.

A thought strikes me. "Baby, will you kill *anyone* I ask you to?"

He tilts his head inquisitively. "Who do you have in mind?"

CHAPTER NINE

KLAUS, MICK, AND the others are working at their stations, and they don't notice me sneaking in behind them. I reach the bathroom door.

"Can you get it open?" I ask Lazarus.

He hits the door with his palm and it blasts off the hinges. My old boss leaps off his porcelain throne. "What—what's going—Neil? What the fuck!"

"I never got my last paycheck," I say.

"You weren't supposed to leave here alive, you bastard."

"And now, that's my line. By the way, pull your pants up—it's embarrassing."

He pulls them up. "Just you try, fucker. You're nothing. I *own* you."

"Own me? Do you even know how much I make now? I'm in the big leagues. You're an ant on my shoe."

"You're the ant, Neil. A worker ant, pretending you're the queen. But people can't change what they are, not really. You'll find that out the hard way."

"You're not the first one to tell me that, and you're wrong," I say. "Your turn, Lazarus."

"What is a baby going to—"

The baby pounces and slits the boss's throat. He claws at his bleeding neck, falls on the toilet, goes limp, and shits.

"Maybe you should have kept the pants off, after all," I say. "Nice job, as usual, Lazarus."

I give him a high five. A second passes before it hits me

what I did. I look at the hand and gasp, jumping back as if I can somehow escape my own appendage. "I . . . I . . . "

I *touched* him. No Hazmat suit or anything. And I feel . . . okay.

The boss is only the first on the list. Next up is the man who bullied me as a kid and testified against me in court—Bobby Denton.

He lives in a shantytown of a trailer park at the south end of town. I have no difficulty picking out his trailer—he's painted it a bombastic red and yellow, the name "Bobby Denton" sprayed on in black. Without bothering to knock, I enter.

The smell hits first, a rancid mix of garbage, rot, and excrement. Trash dominates every surface.

"Hey!" A woman shouts from a derelict couch left of the door. I'd guess she's about thirty, but she looks fifty, and morbidly obese. She takes a hit off a crack pipe and glares at me. "Who is you! You can't just barge in a person's home!"

"Bobby here?" I ask.

"Fuck if I know. Probably out cheatin' with some *bitch*." She takes another hit off the pipe and reaches for the table in front of her, but her enormous arm falls short. "Damn. Grab the remote for me, would you?"

"No. Sit up and get it yourself."

"Fuck you," she says, then grimaces. "Damn. My cooter's hurtin' like a bitch all the sudden."

My eyes fall to her crotch. A fleshy dome pokes through the hem of her skirt.

"Ah!" she shrieks. "Fuck! Goddamn!"

A tiny, pudgy face emerges. She's giving birth.

"*Shiiiiiiiiiiiiiit!*"

The baby squirts onto the couch, crying.

"Damn," she gasps. "I didn't even know that one was

in there." She takes a hit off the pipe. "Well kid, now that you're here, you wanna fetch the remote for me?"

Bobby Denton rushes out of the back room to the right, seeming not to notice me as he storms to the couch. He's a mountain of a man with a gym-rat physique, arms covered in tattoos. "What's all this cryin', damnit!" he roars. He sees the baby. "Bitch! You had *another*? I told you not to have any more!"

"It ain't my fault Bobby, they just keep comin' out!"

He punches her in the face with his brick-sized fist. "Bitch! Stupid fuckin' *bitch!* I know this can't be *my* fault, I wash the condom out real good every time!" He turns to the baby. "And you! Little fuckin' shit, you're the last thing we need right now!" He kicks the baby and the baby cries harder. "Quit cryin'! This is life! You gotta learn to put up with being kicked around a little!"

He kicks it again and again. As he's doing this, another child—three or four years old perhaps—comes out of a door to the left. The child picks up what appears to be a chicken bone off the floor, puts it in his mouth, and starts to choke.

"Hey, your kid . . . " I say.

Bobby whirls to face me. "The fuck! Neil?"

"Your kid's cho—"

Never mind. He's not choking anymore—he's dead.

"You're a pathetic piece of shit, Bobby," I say, "And I'm here to kill you."

"You're the one who's gonna die, retard," he says. He makes a fist and windmills his arm a few times, gearing up for a punch. Before he can, Lazarus pounces from my side, latching on below his shoulder.

"What the!" Bobby shakes his arm, trying to shake Lazarus off. "What the hell! Get it off me!"

Lazarus seizes his elbow and twists. *Snap.* Bobby screams. Lazarus climbs over his shoulder and seizes his neck. *Snap.* Bobby doesn't scream this time.

His wife does.

"Quiet!" I shout at her.

She screams louder.

"Please! Quiet! Lady, we did you a *favor*!"

She doesn't stop. Lazarus lasers her gut, and she shuts up. A faint cry draws me to the back of the couch. I recoil, hand shooting to my mouth as a small bit of bile climbs my throat and dribbles out.

A child is on the floor, decapitated by the laser.

No. It's not the first time I've seen a dead child. But it's the first time the child's dead because of me. I only came here for Bobby, not . . . I didn't want *this*.

My whole body's cold. It's like I've suddenly woken from a dream, and the person I was in it is someone I don't recognize. What in the world have I been doing? Since when have I ever been a murderer?

On the couch, the mother's still screaming. Even though she's dead . . .

No. The sound's not coming from her. Blue and red lights flash through the window.

"Let's turn ourselves in," I say to Lazarus. But he's not there.

I open the door just in time to be showered in blood and gore as the baby's laser eviscerates a pair of cops.

CHAPTER TEN

HEAD HURTS LIKE HELL Mouth dry. Can't see—blindfolded.

Fuck. I've been kidnapped again. Must've been shot with a tranquilizer.

The blindfold is removed. I blink against the harsh, sudden light of a hanging lamp. Black spots swim across my vision, but they dissipate as my eyes adjust. I'm tied to a chair in an otherwise empty concrete room. In front of me is a set of stairs, a wooden door at the top.

The remover of the blindfold walks around the chair. It's Connor.

"Connor. You bastard."

He slaps the side of my head. It feels like a cast-iron pan, not a hand. Agony explodes through my skull.

"You fucking idiot," he says. "I don't know if you know this, Neil, but what we do is highly illegal. We can't have people who work for us draw heat on our operation by *murdering cops.*"

"Is it too late to say I'm sorry?"

He slaps me again. A Milky Way's worth of stars bursts across my vision with a healthy dose of pain. "Bring that thing down," Connor says.

The door at the top of the stairs opens, and a man in a black mask enters. In his arms is Lazarus, wrapped in chains. A metal plate covers his eyes.

"Let him go," I snarl.

"I know about you, you know," Connor says. "Who

doesn't? You were all over the news. Baby hater, they called you. What changed?"

"Eat shit," I snarl.

"You're a strange man, getting attached to such a horrific abomination of nature. Then again, I suppose you two are perfect for each other."

"You won't be able to restrain him for long. You have no idea how powerful he is."

"We do know, as a matter of fact. From the moment we hired you, we were well aware of his potential. We put our best scientists to work developing technology capable of subduing him. Those are no ordinary chains; he'll never break free of them. And the plate over his eyes will block his lasers—we tested it."

"Scientists?" I'm beginning to understand the scope of what I've done. This is no small organization I've pissed off. "Just who are you people?"

"We're a group you never should have fucked with," Connor says. His phone rings. He takes it from his pocket. "Hello?" I can't hear the person on the other end, but Connor frowns. "Are you sure, boss? All right. It's safe to come down." He hangs up. "Don't know why, but the boss wants to see you."

The door opens again, and a man descends the steps. It's the weird interviewer with the bowling ball-shaped head and the nose the size of an orange, the one whose office smelled like cheese and who had a thing for eggs.

"You've got to be kidding me," I say. "*This* is your boss?"

"Eggs," the boss says.

"Address him with respect," Connor says.

"This killing I've been doing. Has it just been to eliminate your competition?" I ask.

"Mac 'n' cheese," the boss says.

"Why are you here if you're not going to say anything that makes sense?"

Connor rams the heel of his boot into my stomach. *"You! Will! Address him! With! Respect!"*

MY WEIRD NIGHTMARE BABY

I turn back to the boss. "Okay," I wheeze, breath knocked out of me by the kick. "I apologize, O venerable one."

Connor narrows his eyes, but lets the sarcasm pass. He looks at the boss. "What do you want us to do?" he asks.

The boss sticks a finger up his left nostril.

Connor nods and turns to the masked man. "Do it," he says.

The man produces a syringe.

"Wait," Connor says. "Not yet. I'm not done talking to this asshole."

"What's in there? Poison?" I ask. "You can't kill him, I've tried."

"Didn't I explain this to you?" Connor says. "Our scientists have worked out everything."

"You'd be killing an infant."

"That thing? It's no infant. We both know that." He bends forward, bringing his face close to mine. "You're a fool, Neil. You think you're hot shit because you have a fucked up demon baby that shoots lasers. Well, you're not—you're nothing. *We* gave you the opportunity to be more. And you threw it away. Remember that."

"Please don't kill him," I say.

"Why shouldn't we?"

"Because . . . " What could I say?

Think about how you ended up here. There has to be some way to talk your way out.

I'd been fed up with it all. Society, the people in it, everything. With all that power suddenly dumped in my lap, I lost sight of myself. I'd earned my place in this chair. The therapist, the fat man and Jim, my boss . . . they were all . . .

"You're right," I say. "You're right about me."

"You think acknowledging that will fix this?" Connor asks.

No. But it helps me understand what I need to do. I deserve to be here, but Lazarus doesn't.

"He had nothing to do with it," I say. "I killed those cops."

Connor laughs. "You? All by yourself? Impossible."

"I told him to do it! He's just a baby, he doesn't know better. He did as I asked. So do *any*thing you want to me. Torture me, whatever. Just leave him out of it. If you let him live, maybe you can weaponize him—make him work for you, without me as the middleman."

Connor shakes his head. "Thought about that. Too risky." He turns to the masked man with the syringe. "Do it."

"Don't!" I scream.

Bang.

The masked man topples forward. The shooter, a blond man, steps through the door at the top of the stairs.

"Shit!" Connor dives for cover behind my chair. "Not again! Boss, get behind me!"

The boss ducks behind Connor. The gunman approaches.

"Please don't shoot," I say.

"Shoot you? Why would I kill a guy who's tied up?"

"Who are you? A competitor?"

"Disgruntled ex-employee!" Connor shouts. "Fifth goddamn time this month! How'd you find our secret bunker, jackass?"

"The secret bunker behind an unlocked door just to the left of the building's entrance?" the man asks. "Big mystery, isn't it? How about you come out from behind this guy and face me like a man?"

"Gee, I don't know, because you'll shoot me?"

"Gonna shoot you either way. You and that egg-loving bastard."

"How about you *don't* shoot us? Is that a possibility?"

"After you assholes fired me, I lost the ability to pay for my wife's cancer treatments. You know what happened to her? She *died.* You *murdered* her!"

"Take some personal responsibility, man. If you were fired, there was probably a reason for it."

"Egg salad," the boss says.

"Shut up. You die for killing her."

"Free me first?" I suggest.

"Oh. Sure."

He unties me with his free hand, the gun still trained on his targets.

"If you're gonna kill us, get it over with," Connor says.

The man passes my chair, pistol at the ready. The boss launches off the ground like a loaded spring and rams the man's chin, knocking him back. He drops the gun and it clatters to the floor. The boss sprays him with a deluge of bubbly green mucus. "Eggs, bitch! Eggs!" The man groans, drenched in slimy green nose juice. Connor dives for the gun, aims, and fires. The man's skull bursts and oozes blood, the red liquid mixing with the green like Christmas come early.

I'm halfway to the stairs before they see me. "Stop!" Connor yells. The gun goes off, but misses. I scoop up Lazarus and remove the plate from his eyes. His lasers detach Connor's arm from his body. Connor screams, and I exit the room.

Cop lights flash through glass double doors on the right. "You're surrounded!" they shout. "Come out with your hands up!"

I turn left. If anyone saw me at Bobby's trailer, the police will be looking for me. The hallway is littered with bodies, all of them felled by gunshot wounds. The room below must be thoroughly soundproofed for me to have missed all the shooting.

"Stop!" Connor shouts behind me.

I run. A gunman turns a corner and enters the hallway. "You bastards are gonna pay for firing me!" he shouts.

"Are you kidding me?" Connor shouts. "Two in *one day*?"

The man shoots. The baby's laser disintegrates the bullet in midair. The police storm the building, and then— chaos. The shooter fires on the cops, going down in a blaze

of glory. Lazarus's lasers go haywire, slicing ceiling, walls, flesh. Agonized screams from every direction. I run, my focus solely on getting Lazarus and myself to safety.

I find an exit and leave the building. Outside, the city is in flames. People are shooting, beating, stabbing each other, and smashing everything they can. Corpses lie everywhere.

"Neil!"

Mom is running toward me. A man rushes her with a knife; Lazarus stops him.

"Mom." I gape at her fully healed body. "You're not injured."

"Experimental new surgery," she says. "Good as new, huh?"

"What's going on?" I ask.

"I don't know. Something on the news has got everyone riled up. I wanted to make sure my boys were okay! How's progress coming along on those next grandchildren? I'm not getting any younger, you know."

"Listen, Mom," I say. "I'm sorry. I experienced something that made me reflect on a few things. I've treated you like shit."

"It's okay, sweetie. I—"

A massive green tentacle slams into her. She's sent ragdolling backward, into a brick wall. I run to her. "Mom!"

She's dead.

"*Neeeiiil!*" It's Jimbob. "*I'll kill yooooou!*"

He's bigger and more grotesque than ever. His slimy form towers skyward like a mountain of feces, colossal root-like tentacles spreading outward from the base.

I look at Mom's corpse. Then at Jimbob.

"Lazarus."

Lazarus nods. He turns his eyes to Jimbob.

Red lasers tear into Jimbob's flesh. Green gunk sprays. Jimbob roars loud enough to wake the dead and raises a tentacle. Lasers slice through. The tentacle hits the ground flopping. Lazarus aims again at the main body and continues to fire.

Jimbob explodes. Thousands of greasy globs of flesh are retched outward by the blast, giving me a free shower.

"At least . . . " Jimbob groans. "At least . . . I got to be dentures . . . "

Lazarus turns back to me. "Dead," he says.

The city has fallen silent. A crowd of people approach me. A woman steps to the front. She falls to her knees. "He has killed the king! All hail the new king!"

"Hail the king!" the crowd responds in unison.

"Oh, fuck off," I say.

I pick up Lazarus and walk away.

"He's leaving," the woman says. "He's leaving us!"

People start to shout. The shouts turn to screams. The screams are drowned out by gunshots. I continue to walk. I walk all the way to the slums. The violence which has consumed the city hasn't reached here; it never does.

A body is being dragged from a tent. I face no objections as I lift the tent's flap and enter. Inside, there's nothing but a rolled-up sleeping bag and an overturned box with a candlestick on top. I take a seat on the bag and put Lazarus down beside me.

"We're home," I say.

It isn't much. But as long as I have my son, it'll do.

ABOUT THE AUTHOR

Riley Odell is an autistic neurodiversity advocate and writer of horror, comedy, bizarro, and stories about autism. His second horror collection, *Vile Visions Volume 2*, was nominated for a 2025 Wonderland Award, celebrating superior achievement in bizarro fiction. He edited and published *Divergent Realms: Science Fiction and Fantasy Stories About Neurodivergence*, an anthology of fourteen stories about neurodivergent characters, written by neurodivergent writers. He is also the madman responsible for *Bizarro Circus of Madness*, an anthology of twenty-one bizarro fiction stories. He lives in Fort Collins, Colorado, with his wife Jamie and their two pet children, a dog named Sadie and a rabbit named Newton.